Festive Romances in Early Modern Drama

Nostalgia for Ancient Hospitality and
Wish-fulfillment Fantasy in Mobile Society

Sumiko Maehara

Kwansei Gakuin University Press

Festive Romances in Early Modern Drama:

Nostalgia for Ancient Hospitality
and
Wish-fulfillment Fantasy in Mobile Society

Sumiko Maehara

Kwansei Gakuin University Press

Festive Romances in Early Modern Drama :
Nostalgia for Ancient Hospitality
and Wish-fulfillment Fantasy in Mobile Society

Copyright © 2009 by Sumiko Maehara

All rights reserved.

No part of this book may be reproduced in any form or by any means without permission in writing from the author.

Kwansei Gakuin University Press
1-1-155 Uegahara, Nishinomiya, Hyogo, 662-0891, Japan
ISBN: 978-4-86283-044-9

Acknowledgements

I owe thanks to many, for their scholarly help, encouragement, advice, and friendship. The greatest debt is to my supervisor, Prof. Hiroshi Ozawa, for his valuable advice, his meticulous criticism of each chapter, his encouragement, and his patience. Without his support, this would never have been written. I owe immeasurable thanks to Emeritus Prof. Takashi Sasayama for his stimulating supervision during my years as a doctoral student and for his constant support in the completion of this dissertation.

Contents

Introduction		7
I.	**Festive Representations in Early Modern England**	
	1. Decline of Popular Festivals	11
	2. Saturnalian Feast	15
	3. Lamentation of Decaying Hospitality	27
II.	**Late Elizabethan Entertainments**	
	1. *The Old Wives Tale*	43
	2. *Summer's Last Will and Testament*	61
III.	**Ancient Folkloric Romances**	
	1. *George a Greene, the Pinner of Wakefield*	72
	2. *Mucedorus*	87
	3. *The Seven Champions of Christendom*	93
IV.	**Shakespeare's Romances**	
	1. *Pericles*	103
	2. *The Winter's Tale*	119
Conclusion		133
Notes		137
Works Cited		141
Index		157

Introduction

This dissertation focuses on several romance plays, in which festive elements are predominant. C. L. Barber suggests in his *Shakespeare's Festive Comedies* that festive elements create the psychological dynamics "through release to clarification" (4). Barber's theory is based on the premise that there are analogies between the comic dramatic forms and the Saturnalian rituals. However, Barber excludes Shakespeare's last plays from his study, although they are closely related to festivals, as seen in the sheep-shearing in *The Winter's Tale*, and also have a happy ending like comedies. Barber's research indirectly suggests that festive romances have a quite different dramatic effect from that of festive comedies.

The definition of 'romances' is extensive, covering historical romance, heroic romance, chivalric romance and so forth. They are so-called 'a mixed genre,' which is a blend of tragedy and comedy. They are usually set in distant locations with a wish-fulfillment happy ending. However, romances are most unique in their techniques to break illusion and detach the audience's attention from the action of the drama. A bear's unexpected appearance on stage in *The Winter's Tale* and Gower's Chorus in *Pericles* are typical examples. Critics have long discussed the blatant devices inherent in romance plays, and it is generally agreed that such a contrivance is an attempt to give the audience a larger collective vision of the world, rather than to represent the mimesis itself (Colie 21). In other words, the fiction created on the stage serves as a mirror of offstage reality.

The plays examined in the following chapters embrace many festive elements that are reminiscent of folk rituals in pre-Reformation England. Offstage, however, such ancient customs almost died out under Elizabeth's reign, because they were attacked by radical reformers and also regulated by the State, which was in the process of establishing Protestant national uniformity. Considering this background, festive representations in the theaters must have been outdated for the contemporary audience.

It is often suggested that the spirit of the festival still survived after the Reformation, and that Elizabethan festive drama was the remnants of popular cultural tradition. In fact, people continued to show nostalgia for the ancient festivities. However, the festivals also had a social function, in addition to releasing people from their daily order: making a reconciliatory and consolidating relationship between the rich and the poor, if it was only a temporal one. For example, making a feast for the poor on festive occasions, an act known as hospitality, was highly respected. In contemporary documents, hospitality was generally regarded as a duty of the landed nobility and gentry. However, the custom rapidly declined during the early modern period, reflecting the socioeconomic change of the time. Circulation of money and a capitalist value made the existing hierarchical social order fluid and mobile.

If festive romances serve to give the audience a collective vision of the world, the plays discussed in the following chapters seem to be more relevant to the socioeconomic context than the popular custom itself. The aim of this dissertation is to explore a common perspective represented in the festive romances, and to reconsider Shakespeare's Romances from that perspective.

In the first chapter, I look at the historical background in which popular festivals declined, and illustrate the close relationship between festivals and hospitality, the origin of which goes back to the ancient Saturnalia. In addition, several discourses of early modern England are examined to show lamentation of the decaying hospitality and nostalgia for the good old days, which were frequently represented in the contemporary documents.

In the second chapter, two late Elizabethan entertainments, *The Old Wives Tale* and *Summer's Last Will and Testament* are discussed. In these plays, festive elements are predominant. However, the dramatic structure of the plays is so unique that critics have long considered them difficult to interpret. First, the plot is inconsistent, with a medley of miscellaneous motifs. Secondly, the narrator frequently transgresses the boundary of dramatic action and story-telling framework. These problematic aspects are reconsidered in relation to the primitive structure of old folk drama as well as the medley structure of ancient satire.

In the third chapter, three ancient folkloric romances are examined. *George a Greene, the Pinner of Wakefield* has long been grouped into Robin Hood plays, which were the popular repertoires of London theaters in the 1590s. However, as seen in the shoemakers' episode, the play can also be a wish-fulfillment fantasy of the commonalty. In *Mucedorus* and *The Seven Champions of Christendom*, the matter of birth and breed is frequently questioned by the clownish characters. They satirically allude to contemporary mobile classes, and offstage reality is skillfully fused into the ancient folkloric romances.

In the last chapter, I reconsider Shakespeare's *Pericles* and *The Winter's Tale*. In *Pericles*, Gower's Chorus is deliberately archaic and reminiscent of a medieval moral story. However, his chorus has manifold connotations directly reflecting contemporary society. First, the issue of hospitality is symbolically presented before and after Gower's second Chorus. Secondly, social satires included in the brothel scenes are significant. Wealthy gentlemen's dishonesty is highly caricatured, but Gower's moralistic Chorus tactfully makes it less offensive. In *The Winter's Tale*, the Shepherd's subplot is examined. The Shepherd obtains both wealth and status by finding a deserted baby and gold, and the seemingly innocent tale symbolically reflects the upward mobility of contemporary capitalist society. In addition, garments and apparel are particularly important in the play, serving as a vehicle of one's shifting identity. Sumptuary Laws of Apparel, frequently issued under Elizabeth, were finally repealed in 1604. It is highly probable that sumptuous fashion was prevalent and social cross-dressing was common off stage. Against this background, allegorical meaning of garment/status is also studied.

I

Festive Representations in Early Modern England

1. Decline of Popular Festivals

Many Elizabethan plays feature a festive scene, which is reminiscent of rural festivals widely held in pre-Reformation England. Sheep-shearing in *The Winter's Tale* is a good example of this. In the pastoral celebration, Perdita, who is the queen of the feast, extends generous hospitality to her guests, and reminds the audience of the harmonious relationship in the communities of yore. Thomas Nashe's *Summer's Last Will and Testament* is another example, in which a personified character Ver appears with Morris Dancers and vividly demonstrates the mirth of the May festival. In *Shakespeare's Festive World*, François Laroque illustrates popular festivals, which are frequently referred to in contemporary dramas, such as Twelfth Night, Plough Monday, Shrove Tuesday, St. George, May Day, Midsummer and Christmas. His research is based on preceding surveys conducted by E. K. Chambers (*Mediaeval* 1: 89–418), Charles Read Baskervill ("Dramatic" 19–87), C. L. Barber (3–57) and Glynne Wickham (128–44). It is quite probable that the Elizabethan audiences were familiar with all of these customs.

In the latter half of the 16th century, however, popular festivals were under fierce attack offstage by enthusiastic Protestants, because most of the popular customs derived from pagan or medieval catholic rituals. Philip Stubbes' *The Anatomie of Abuses* is the most frequently quoted as the evidence of the attack. The following is the denunciation of immoral behavior in the May festival:

> [...] Against Maie day, Whitsunday, or some
> other time of the yeare, euery Parish, Towne,
> and village, assemble themselues together, both
> men, women and children, olde and young, euen
> all indifferently: and either going all togither, or
> diuiding themselues into companies, they goe
> some to the woods, and groues, some to the hils
> and mountaines, some to one place, some to an-
> other, where they spende all the night in pleasant
> pastimes, and in the morning they returne bring-
> ing with them Birch boughes, and branches of
> trees, to deck their assemblies withal. [...]
> But their chiefest iewel they bring
> from thence is the *Maie-poale*, which they bring
> home with great veneration, [...] And then fal they to
> banquet and feast, to leape and daunce about it,
> as the Heathen people did, at the dedication of
> their Idolles, whereof this is a perfect patterne, or
> rather the thing it selfe. I haue heard it crediblie
> reported (and that *viua voce*) by men of great
> grauity, credite, and reputation, that of fourtie,
> threescore, or a hundred Maides, going to the
> wood ouernight, there haue scarecely the third
> part of them returned home againe vndefiled.
> (209–10: 5726–37, 5741–43, 5757–66)

Stubbes' *Anatomie* is a fiction, in which unpleasant manners and customs are compiled from a puritanical perspective. Historians often call it "complaint literature" (Stubbes 19–23; Hutton 128). As Barber points out, the description above is possibly overstated by Stubbes, who is well known for his "shrewd journalism" (22). However, it is notable that as many as thirty-five tracts against popular merry-making, including Stubbes' *Anatomie*, were published during the reign of Elizabeth I (Hutton 128). Most of the authors were clergymen and the laity, and their discussion was centered upon the observance of the Sabbath. They denounced drinking and dancing on holy Sundays, when people had to abstain from any kind of recreation as well as from work (Chambers *Elizabethan* 1:253–56; Malcolmson 5–14; Goring 3–28; Hutton 128–34).

The regulation proposed upon the popular festivals was being tightened not only by the radical reformers, but also by the State, which was in the process of establishing Protestant national uniformity. The first reform was made by Henry VIII, who claimed to be the supreme head of the Church of England, and abrogated a large number of feasts and restricted the celebration of holy days. The prohibition of the pageant of Saint John's Day, namely Midsummer Watch in 1539 is well known. The Reformation that followed under Edward VI was more drastic than Henry's. A series of injunctions against festive ceremonies was issued between 1547 and 1548, including the suppression of Corpus Christi. Edward insisted that religious holidays should be celebrated only for honoring God and edifying his congregations, as seen in the 'Act for the Keeping of Holy Days and Fasting Days,' which was passed in his parliament in 1552. Under the Catholic monarch Queen Mary, however, some of the abolished customs were revived, and they were still observed in the 1560s. Churchwardens' accounts show that the popular festivities took place more frequently in the 1560s than in the preceding half-century.[1] In spite of that, the popular festivals rapidly declined during Elizabeth's reign. In the 1570s, Corpus Christi was permanently halted in Coventry, York, Chester and Wakefield. In the 1580s, Maypoles were banned in Doncaster, Lincoln, Banbury, Canterbury, Shrewsbury and in many other places. Midsummer Watch disappeared almost in the same period. In the 1590s, local plays customarily acted by craft guilds on Hock Tuesday, St George's Day and Midsummer were largely discontinued. Most other traditional folk customs, like church ales and Plough Monday gatherings were officially abolished by the end of Elizabeth's reign, though they were privately maintained in a few places (Cressy 1–33; Laroque *Shakespeare's* 74–154; Wasson 70–78; Hutton 69–152).[2]

Historians find it difficult to specify the reason why the popular festivals declined so rapidly under Elizabeth. There were probably several interrelated factors that made them disappear (Goring 5; Hutton 111–12). First, the increasing importance of liturgical ceremonies is pointed out. As Keith Wrightson suggests in his *English Society 1580–1680*, the Reformation largely took root at the parish level in the last decade of the 16th century (199–221). It is assumed that liturgical ceremonies gradually became more respected than the popular festivals. Secondly, the Accession Day of Elizabeth I, which was newly created as a national festival, is significant (Strong "Popular" 86–103; Cressy 50–57; Laroque *Shakespeare's* 64–73; Hutton 146–152). Elizabeth was actually enthroned on 17 November, but her Accession Day was fixed at the beginning of May, when people had previously enjoyed notorious Morris dances around the Maypole. Furthermore, the royal festival was celebrated throughout the country by ringing bells and holding processions, closely connected with the Rogation ceremonies (Strong "Popular" 88–91). As a courtly event, medieval tournaments were revived to commemorate her accession. Some critics suggest that the chivalrous element was utilized so that it could supplant old religious ceremonies of the Catholic calendar (Yates 98–102; Laroque *Shakespeare's* 72). In addition, summer progresses were regularly held at least during her first twenty years, and pageants and banquets were sumptuously provided in country houses. As Roy C. Strong (*Cult*) and Frances A. Yates have illustrated in detail, Elizabeth was often identified with Astraea and deified as the Virgin Queen restoring the Golden Age. Thus, the enthusiasm for the national festival as well as the Reformation gradually attenuated the old community observances.

If the customs of popular festivals virtually died out under Elizabeth, a question remains why popular festivals were often represented in London theaters even after the 1590s. Critics and historians have generally agreed that the spirit of the popular festivals still survived in the theater, though the customs themselves were gradually discontinued by the end of the 16th century (Baskervill *Elizabethan* 3–369; K. Thomas "Place" 77–81; Weimann 15–48, 167–77). This assumption is supported by the high popularity of jig and clowning performed by Richard Tarlton and William Kempe. The popular tradition is also found in structural and verbal elements of folk plays abundantly used in the works of Shakespeare and his contemporaries. It is undeniable that the festive elements in the theater were the remnants of popular cultural tradition. However, it draws my interest how the original audiences perceived the representations of the festivals, which were outdated in the real world. What kind of significance did they find in the festive representations in the theater?

2. Saturnalian Feast

To discuss the issue at stake, it is necessary to look at C. L. Barber's viewpoint, as illustrated in his *Shakespeare's Festive Comedy*. He was the first critic to analyze the socio-historical meaning of the Elizabethan festive drama, and has had much influence on the later criticism. Barber observes that there is a common function between popular festival and festive comedy: they both serve as a means of releasing people from their daily orders. Barber particularly refers to ancient Roman Saturnalia, which is well known for the custom whereby the roles of master and servants are temporarily inverted. Northrop Frye also notices a parallel between the Saturnalian rituals and literary comic forms, but he develops the idea further in his archetypal criticism.[3] Barber's argument centers on the much narrower context: a Tudor holiday custom, the "Lord of Misrule."

The Lord of Misrule is a well-known English Saturnalian entertainment, whose earliest occasion is recorded at the court of Edward I in

1277 (Welsford 199–219; Weimann 20–30; Billington 30–54). This custom was probably popular until the early Elizabethan period; Robert Dudley acted the misrule lord at the Inner Temple in 1561. According to contemporary writings, such as Philip Stubbes' (206–09) and John Stow's (122–23), the misrule lord, namely a mock king, was usually elected before the festive season and presided over the festivities. However, the misrule entertainments sometimes caused disorderly conduct, and were finally abolished at the end of the 16th century, as well as other popular festivals. Even after the prohibition, however, a Saturnalian entertainment entitled *The Christmas Prince* was held at St. John's College, Oxford in 1607. The text shows that the festivity was totally benign, because it was no more than the old custom revived after a thirty-year interval:

> This motion for that the person of a Prince or Lorde of the Revells had not bine knowen amongst them for thirty yeares before, & so consequentlye the danger, charge, and trouble of such iestinge was cleane forgotten was p'sentlye allowed, and greedilye apprehended of all.
>
> (Boas 4)

In spite of this apology, the record of the performance itself proves that the spirit of Saturnalia was still alive in 17th-century England.

Looking at these social contexts, Barber focuses on the plays with holiday motifs, like *Love's Labour's Lost*, *A Midsummer Night's Dream* and *Twelfth Night*, and illustrates the analogies between the comic dramatic forms and the Saturnalian rituals:

> The saturnalian pattern appears in many variations, all of which involve inversion, statement and counterstatement, and a basic movement which can be summarized in the formula, through release to clarification.
>
> (4)

Barber notes "the tendency for Elizabethan comedy to *be* a saturnalia, rather than to *represent* saturnalian experience" (36). In other words, the Elizabethan theater became a replacement for the popular festivals after the Reformation abolished them.

Barber's argument is full of great insight. Particularly, the presupposition that the festive elements create the psychological dynamics "through release to clarification" is important. This theory accidentally overlaps with Mikhail Bakhtin's great research, *Rabelais and His World*, which was first translated into English in 1968. Bakhtin postulates that the medieval carnival is derived from the Roman Saturnalia, in which normal orders were temporarily inverted in the festive merriment. However, Bakhtin's perspective on festive inversion is quite different from Barber's "through release to clarification" theory. Bakhtin insists that carnivalesque subversion is more radical and liberated than a reveling of "the official feast," which is designed to authorize existing social orders. According to Bakhtin, "Carnival was the true feast of time, the feast of becoming, change, and renewal. It was hostile to all that was immortalized and completed" (7–11).

Bakhtin's study made an epoch in literary criticism, accelerating heated discussions on carnivalesque. Among the critics of Renaissance drama, 'the world upside down' has become a dominant perspective when the festive elements are discussed. Particularly, New Historicists, who are exclusively concerned with the subversive elements in the theater found a good fortress in Bakhtin's radical perspective. They reduce Barber's argument to a merely conservative "safety valve," and debate whether the Saturnalian elements in plays are really subversive or not, drawing on their original formula of "subversion and containment." Michael Bristol's *Carnival and Theatre* is a typical example of Bakhtinian study. In this research, Bristol criticizes Barber's formula "through release to clarification," and insists that "release" is not followed by a "clarification" but a "reaffirmation of the *status quo*" (30–32). For another example, Manfred Phister argues that "there is the surprising structural similarity between comic discourse and revolutionary discourse,": "they both have the effect of reversing established evaluations, levelling down hierarchical distinctions and projecting an alternative 'world upside down'" (27). However, Phister's argument is quite different from Bristol's. Phister divides Shakespeare's festive discourses into two: Saturnalian inversion in early comedies and a thoroughly carnivalized version in problematic comedies or late plays. Phister concludes that Saturnalian inversions are not really subversive but "these confusions are always quickly defused, as they are contained within an over-ruling framework of a benign and flexible order, which puts them back into perspective" (39).

Admittedly, festive elements can be a metaphor of rebellion, violence and potentially radical/safe inversions of hierarchies as the New Historicists observe.[4] However, it is too simplistic to look at the Saturnalia only from one aspect, because the Saturnalia originally had several functions over and above the hierarchal inversion. As James G. Frazer illustrates the diversified versions of the ancient Saturnalia in *The Golden Bough* (630–41), the Saturnalia did suspend any kind of social reality, not only master and servants. For example, it was applied to the relationship between the rich and the poor.

This assumption is reinforced by Lucian's *Ta pros Kronon* whose Latin title is *Saturnalia*. It is generally agreed that the Greek Cronia and the Roman Saturnalia are identical because both of them commemorate the god of agriculture, Cronus/Saturn (Howatson 509; James 175–77; Hammond 955). The work consists of dialogic discourse between the Priest and Cronus over the "laws" of Cronia/Saturnalia. The Priest repeatedly complains of inequality between the rich and the poor, and asks Cronus for more wealth. Cronus says that the equality can be realized only in the Saturnalia, and it is nothing more than the suspension of reality. However, Cronus finally writes a letter to the rich, and bids them to give generous gifts to the poor:

> The poor have recently written me complaining that you don't let them share what you have, and, to be brief, they asked me to make the good things common to all and let everyone

have his bit. [...]
   Oh yes, the dinners and their dining with you—they asked me to add this to my letter, that at present you gorge alone behind locked doors, and, if ever at long intervals you are willing to entertain any of them, there is more annoyance than good cheer in the dinner, and most of what happens is done to hurt them—that business of not drinking the same wine as you, for instance—goodness! how ungenerous that is! [...] There are many more like complaints of meanness, complaints that bring little credit to gentlemen. In fact the pleasantest thing, more in keeping with conviviality, is equality, and a controller of the feast presides over your banquets just so that all can have an equal share.

(Lucian p. 129–33)

The discussion above illuminates the reconciliatory and consolidating relationship between the rich and the poor, not a radical subversion of master and servants (Nauta 184–86). Moreover, the fictional setting of the work is law-giving by Cronus/Saturn; the basic concept of the Saturnalia is entirely concerned with the reconciliation between the rich and the poor.

Another example is Statius' *The Kalends of December*, which is included in Book I of *Silvae*. The following passage suggests that the feast is held on December 1st, preceding the Saturnalia:

   Father Phoebus and stern Pallas and you Muses, away with you, take a holiday! We will call you back on Janus' Kalends. Let Saturn join me free of his chains and wine-soaked December and laughing Jollity and wanton Jests, as I relate merry Caesar's joyous day and the tipsy feast.

(Book I. 6:89)[5]

The feast is an occasion of reciprocity between the different social classes, allowing gift-giving and convivial conversation while they shared the same meal:

> Antiquity, compare if you will the ages of ancient Jove and the golden time: not so freely did wine flow then, not thus would harvest forestall the tardy year. Every order eats at one table: children, women, populace, Knights, Senate. Freedom has relaxed reverence. Nay, you yourself (which of the gods could thus invite, which accept invitation?) entered the feast along with us. Now everyone, be he rich or poor, boasts of dining with the leader.
>
> (Book I. 6:91)

It is a common view that the ancient Saturnalian tradition survived in the Christian era, probably as a hybrid of Greek and Roman cultures. However, the importance of celebration may have changed according to the religious and cultural backgrounds. In post-Reformation England, the nature of festivals was likely to be less radical and liberated than that of the Mediterranean area (Welsford 203–05; Burke *Popular* 191–92). As seen in the two classical works quoted above, the reciprocity between the rich and the poor is one of the key elements of the Saturnalia. It is assumed that Elizabethan England put no less emphasis on that custom than on the Lord of Misrule.

In fact, making a feast for the poor on festive occasions, an act known as hospitality, was highly respected in Elizabethan England. Felicity Heal, the author of *Hospitality in Early Modern England*, demonstrates that hospitality was one of the highest public concerns especially between the 1580s and the 1630s. Quoting contemporary documents such as conduct books, advice, sermons and writings on secular ethics, Heal suggests that hospitality was generally regarded as a duty of the landed nobility and gentry. Anyone who visited the household, regardless of social status or the degree of acquaintance, was entertained to be given food, drink and accommodation. Moreover, hospitality was most remarkable in festive celebrations like Christmas, harvest and dedication events such as the Wake (Heal "Idea" 66–93; Heal *Hospitality* 1–22; K. Thomas *Religion* 663–64).

As charitable conducts are repeatedly preached in the Gospels and Epistles in the New Testament, hospitality is rightly compatible with the Christian conception of beneficence.[6] Above all, Matthew (25:35–36), Romans (12:13) and Hebrews (13:2) were frequently quoted as counsels to householders, who had the duty of entertaining the poor (Heal "Idea" 72). In *The Book of Common Prayer* reissued in 1571, the following article on alms-giving is included:

> XXXVIII. Of Christian men's goods, which are not common: The riches and the goods of Christians are not common, as touching the right, title, and possession of the same, as certain Anabaptists do falsely boast. Notwithstanding every man ought, of such things as he possesseth, liberally to give alms to the poor, according to his ability.
>
> (Harrison 21)

Books of Homilies also played an important role in Elizabethan parish life, spreading the reformed religion among the ordinary people. In the second *Books of Homilies* published in 1571, an article "of Alms-deeds" is included (Harrison 22–30). Even to the illiterate, the virtue of merciful giving was repeatedly preached from the pulpit (Harrison 79–83).

Among many documents showing the correlation between festival and hospitality, the following two calendric works are particularly worth noting. The first one is Thomas Tusser's didactic verse, *Five Hundred Points of Good Husbandry*. It was a Tudor best-seller, which was reprinted and enlarged after the first publication entitled *A Hundredth Goode Pointes of Husbandrie* (1557). The record shows us the details of Elizabethan agrarian life, including many pieces of advice. Tusser refers to the openness of Christmas feast: "At Christmas we banket, the rich with the poore, / who then (but the miser) but openeth [h]is doore?" (Tusser 62).

In "A Description of Housekeeping" the author suggests that good housekeeping is essential to entertain the poor especially at Christmas, though hospitality should be maintained all year around:

> WHAT then of this talent, while here we remaine,
>   to studie to yeeld it to God with a gaine?
> And that shall we doo, if we doo it not hid,
>   but use and bestow it, as Christ doth us bid.
>
> What good to get riches by breaking of sleepe,
>   but (having the same) a good house for to keepe?
> Not onely to bring a good fame to thy doore,
>   but also the praier to win of the poore.
>
> Of all other dooings house keeping is cheefe,
>   for daily it helpeth the poore with releefe;
> The neighbour, the stranger, and all that have neede,
>   which causeth thy dooings the better to speede.
>
> Though harken to this we should ever among,
>   yet cheefly at Christmas, of all the yeare long.
> Good cause of that use may appeare by the name,
>   though niggerly niggards doo kick at the same.
>   (61)

Hospitality is the gift to "the poor, the neighbor, the stranger and all that have need." In "August Husbandry," how to entertain husbandmen at harvest time is suggested:

> In harvest time, harvest folke, servants and all,
>   should make all togither good cheere in the hall:
> And fill out the black boule of bleith to their song,
>   and let them be merrie all harvest time long.

> Once ended thy harvest, let none be begilde,
>   please such as did helpe thee, man, woman, and childe.
> Thus dooing, with alway such helpe as they can,
>   thou winnest the praise of the labouring man.
>   (Tusser 124)

More than half a century after the first publication of Tusser's *Husbandry*, Nicholas Breton compiled a unique book of calendric pastimes, *Fantastickes* (1626), which consists of the descriptions of twelve hours, twelve months and some special days, including Christmas. The following passage quoted from "Christmas day" depicts generous entertainment at Christmas:

> It is now Christmas, and not a Cup of drinke must passe without a Caroll, the Beasts, Fowle, and Fish, come to a generall execution, and the Corne is ground to dust for the Bakehouse, and the Pastry: [...] now good cheere and welcome, and God be with you, and I thanke you, and against the new yeare, prouide for the presents: the Lord of Mis-rule is no meane man for his time, and the ghests of the high Table must lacke no Wine [...] In summe, it is a holy time, a duty in Christians, for the remembrance of Christ, and custome among friends, for the maintenance of good fellowship.
>   (Breton *Fantastickes* 11)

However, Breton's description of the Christmas feast seems rather urbanized, compared with Tusser's. Breton does not refer to hospitality to "strangers," but says that Christmas is the custom "among friends, for the maintenance of good fellowship." This may suggest that the modes of hospitality were slightly different between the two ages of Tusser and Breton. Breton also refers to "the Lord of Mis-rule." However, the author's central concern is not over the misrule entertainment which was declined more than thirty years before. In this respect, Heal's argument is quite suggestive. According to Heal, the feast of Christmas was closely linked with the household and the openness of its hospitality. It was this mode of behavior that ensured the continuity in the tradition of the Christmas rejoicings, even at the height of the Commonwealth campaign against the festival (Heal *Hospitality* 354–56). In other words, the Saturnalian custom barely survived in the Protestant culture in the form of the particular mode of entertainment: inviting people to one's household for a meal and drinks with generosity and conviviality.

If the association between festival and hospitality was axiomatic in post-Reformation England, festive representations in the theater must have reminded the original audiences of the hospitality issue. In fact, hospitality is frequently highlighted in festive drama with the manifold connotation. For instance, in the sheep-shearing in *The Winter's Tale*, the Shepherd recollects his dead wife's good hospitality, and scolds his young daughter who does not know the country manner and neglects her homely duties:

> *Shep.* Fie, daughter, when my old wife liv'd, upon
>   This day she was both pantler, butler, cook,
>   Both dame and servant; welcom'd all, serv'd all;
>   Would sing her song, and dance her turn; now here,
>   At upper end o' th' table, now i' th' middle;
>   On his shoulder, and his; her face o' fire
>   With labor, and the thing she took to quench it
>   She would to each one sip. You are retired,
>   As if you were a feasted one, and not
>   The hostess of the meeting. Pray you bid
>   These unknown friends to' us welcome, for it is
>   A way to make us better friends, more known.
>   (4.4. 55–66)[7]

The sheep-shearing was a cordial occasion, in which the sumptuous feast was provided to many visitors so as to maintain the good relationship within the community (Laroque *Shakespeare's* 156–57; Heal "Idea" 87). However, in several late Elizabethan documents, there are debates over the feasts in rural areas. For example, *Questions of Profitable and Pleasant Concernings* (1594), which was dedicated to Robert Devereux, Earle of Essex, denounces "excessiue cost" spent on the "carelesse hospitalitie" and says that a sheep-shearing feast is so luxurious that it costs as much as "three sheapheards wages" (B 4). The original audiences of *The Winter's Tale* probably aware of the specific implications in the Shepherd's comment on hospitality in the pastoral setting above, directly related to the contemporary debates.

This kind of dramatic device is more remarkable in Thomas Nashe's *Summer's Last Will and Testament*. A personified dramatic character, Christmas, appears with Backwinter without singing a carol, and Summer says:

> Christmas, how chance thou com'st not as the rest,
> Accompanied with some musique, or some song?
> A merry Carroll would haue grac't thee well;
> Thy ancestors haue vs'd it heretofore.
>
> (1623–26)

Christmas answers, "I, antiquity was the mother of ignorance" (1627). This may be a reflection of Elizabethan society, in which popular festivals were declining rapidly and merry-making had disappeared. What is more important is Christmas' debate with Summer over the issue of hospitality. Summer asks Christmas why he is reluctant to spend money for entertaining the guests when Christmas is the "god of hospitality." Christmas says that hospitality is "out of fashion" because it prevents good husbandry:

> *Summer.* Why, thou should'st spend, thou should'st not care to get.
> Christmas is god of hospitality.
> *Christmas.* So will he neuer be of good husbandry. I

may say to you, there is many an old god that is now growne
out of fashion. So is the god of hospitality.

(1633–37)

Christmas' comment is not only retrospective but also ironic, because hospitality is one of the most virtuous deeds on Christian moral grounds. It completely contradicts what Tusser advises in his *Five Hundred Points of Good Husbandry*.

Glynn Wickham suggests that the festive representations in Elizabethan plays are both "nostalgic and mocking" in his *The Medieval Theatre*. Referring to the pastoral scene in *The Winter's Tale*, Wickham observes that until the Reformation, music and drama contributed to the development of the folk-festival, and that after the Reformation, the tide began to turn and the professional playwrights borrowed pastoral themes and plots from country revels in both a nostalgic and a mocking vein (149). However, Wickham does not explain how and why the festive representations are "nostalgic and mocking." From a slightly different perspective, Laroque notes burlesque elements in the festive plays of Shakespeare and Beaumont and Fletcher. He suggests that the festive element itself is less significant than the spectacle of festivity revived 'the festival' on the stage. Laroque observes that the theatrical festivity, which was under royal protection, guaranteed that the pleasure of festivity would not be opposed by anyone. Laroque specifies "the Puritans" as the body of the opposition (*Shakespeare's* 186).

The mocking elements in the festive scenes are often interpreted as the playwrights' ironic comments on Puritans, who attacked popular recreations like theater and festivals. However, much more debate may be necessary to determine whether the playwrights were really mocking Puritanism itself. As seen in the two festive scenes quoted above, hospitality is "nostalgically and mockingly" represented as what was missing in Elizabethan society. The allusions to festivals may serve to show the gap between the past and the present. As Heal suggests, if hospitality was a matter of public concern throughout the early modern period, the connotation of hospitality possibly changed under different times and circumstances, reflecting the socio-economic context of the time. Hospitality represented in various ways in the early modern period may deserve further consideration.

3. Lamentation of Decaying Hospitality

While hospitality has never been the central focus in the study of drama, it has been much explored in relation to "country house poems" of the early 17th century. Some of the country house poems, in which landlord's hospitality is thematized, may provide a crucial hint for this research.

Above all, Ben Jonson's "To Penshurst" is exemplified as the most distinguished work of the genre. It is included in the collection of the poems *The Forest*. Jonson published both *The Forest* and *Epigrams* in the 1616 folio of his *Works*, which was awarded a royal pension. When Jonson wrote the poem, the estate belonged to Robert Sidney, Lord Lisle, who was the younger brother of Philip. The main building dates from around 1350, and was passed into the Sidney family in 1552 (McClung 106; Dubrow 153). The poet skillfully and rhetorically focuses on the social function of the great household in the rural community.

In the opening lines, the architectural appearance is referred to:

> Thou art not, Penshurst, built to envious show,
> Of touch, or marble; nor canst boast a row
> Of polished pillars, or a roof of gold:
> Thou has no lantern whereof tales are told,
> Or stair, or courts; but standst an ancient pile,
> And these grudged at, art reverenced the while.
> (1–6)[8]

The house is characteristically defined by negative terms, and markedly contrasted with showy buildings made of "touch or marble" with "polished pillars" or "a roof of gold." In the lines, several critics find the poet's indirect criticism of ostentatious country houses built by powerful noblemen such as William Cecil, Sir Christopher Hatton, Robert Cecil and Thomas Howard (Hibbard "Country" 159–62; McClung 2–3).

The poet also pays tribute to the rich productivity of the estate:

> The lower land, that to the river bends,
> Thy sheep, thy bullocks, kine, and calves do feed:
> The middle grounds thy mares, and horses breed.
> Each bank doth yield thee conies, and the tops,
> Fertile of wood, Ashore, and Sidney's copse,
> To crown thy open table, doth provide
> The purpled pheasant, with the speckled side:
> The painted partridge lies in every field,
> And, for thy mess, is willing to be killed.
> And if the high-swollen Medway fail thy dish,
> Thou hast thy ponds, that pay thee tribute fish:
> Fat, agèd carps, that run into thy net;
>
> (22–33)

Self-sufficient provisions of Penshurst are rhetorically identified with *sponte sua* of the Golden Age, when food was abundantly supplied without any toil. *Sponte sua* is one of the Golden Age motifs frequently used in early modern country house poems (McClung 12–13, 118–22; McBride 102). In Thomas Carew's "To Saxham," a similar motif is found:

> The pheasant, partridge, and the lark,
> Flew to thy house, as to the Ark.
> The willing ox, of himself came
> Home to the slaughter, with the lamb;
> And every beast did thither bring
> Himself, to be an offering.
>
> (21–26)

Another of Jonson's poems "To Sir Robert Wroth" has a direct reference to Saturn's reign, which is unmistakably linked to the Golden Age: "Thus Pan, and Silvane, having had their rites, / Comus puts in, for new delights, / And fills thy open hall with mirth, and cheer, / As if in Saturn's reign it were;"(47–50).

Since nostalgia for the Golden Age is one of the classical conventions, as seen in Virgil's *Georgics* (Book IV),[9] Tibullus' *Elegy* (Book I. iii)[10] and Martial's *Epigrams* (Book X: 29–30),[11] it is most likely that Jonson uses a classical model for his "To Penshurst" (Hibbard "Country" 159; Røstvig I, 60–67; McClung 7–17; McBride 99). Particularly, Martial's *Epigrams*, which is directly echoed in Jonson's *Epigrams* in their variety of length and tone, may be a key to decoding "To Penshurst." In Martial's Book III, an epigram is addressed to Bassus, who is the owner of a magnificent country house located near Rome. However, Bassus is preoccupied with urban life and frequently leaves his household. Thus, his large garden is uncared-for and unproductive. Bassus' pretentious villa is contrasted with Faustinus' rustic house, which is artless but has rich production. Moreover, Faustinus' laborers are willing to work and obey the orders without any supervision. They visit their landlord, bringing the harvest as a gift. In return, Faustinus makes a feast and extends good hospitality to them. In other words, the rich productivity of Faustinus' villa represents *sponte sua* of the Golden Age, contrasted with Bassus' bad housekeeping infected by urban vices.

In a very similar way, Jonson praises the landlord's generosity and unforced labor in Penshurst. Reciprocity between the landowner and their tenants is illuminated:

> And though thy walls be of the country stone,
> They're reared with no man's ruin, no man's groan:
> There's none, that dwell about them, wish them down;
> But all come in, the farmer, and the clown,
> And no one empty-handed, to salute
> Thy lord and lady, though they have no suit.

> Some bring a capon, some a rural cake,
> Some nuts, some apples; some that think they make
> The better cheeses, bring' em; or else send
> By their ripe daughters, whom they would commend
> This way to husbands; and whose baskets bear
> An emblem of themselves, in plum, or pear.
> But what can this (more then express their love)
> Add to thy free provisions, far above
> The need of such? whose liberal board doth flow
> With all that hospitality doth know!
> Where comes no guest, but is allowed to eat,
> Without his fear, and of thy lord's own meat:
> Where the same beer, and bread, and self-same wine
> That is his lordship's, shall be also mine;
>
> (45–64)

This is a completely idealized vision of what Tusser advises in his *Husbandry*. Furthermore, there is a close parallel between Martial's Book III and "To Penshurst" in their endings. Martial reproaches Bassus' villa for being nothing but a "painted villa" (245). The speaker says:

> But *you* [Bassus] have a property near Rome, all elegance and starvation. [...] You feed your vineyard workers with town flour and in time of leisure transport vegetables, eggs, chickens, apples, cheese, must to your painted villa. Should this be called a place in the country or a townhouse out of town?
>
> (p. 243–45)

In "To Penshurst," the speaker is not directly reproachful, but suggests how useless other ostentatious houses are:

> Now, Penshurst, they that will proportion thee
> With other edifices, when they see

> Those proud, ambitious heaps, and nothing else,
> May say, their lords have built, but thy lord dwells.
> (99–102)

Jonson's satiric device is clear in this conclusive ending. In other words, the encomium and the criticism are the opposite side of the same coin in "To Penshurst."

Some of the country house poems more explicitly show the satiric intention. For example, Robert Herrick's *A Panegyric to Sir Lewis Pemberton* directly criticizes the illiberal landlord. The most harsh criticism is in Joseph Hall's "House-keeping's Dead." This work heavily draws on Juvenal's *Fifth Satire*, in which a vulgar host Virro is satirically portrayed because he deliberately serves food of lesser quality to his guest (McClung 42–45; Dubrow 155–56). Hall is one of the most famous Elizabethan satirists, and "House-keeping's Dead" was originally written as the *Second Satire* of Book V of his *Virgidemiae*. However, this work is generally categorized as a country house poem, as Fowler included this in his *The Country House Poems* (39–44). In the following lines, chimneys without smoke are symbolically depicted as a sign of the decaying hospitality.

> Look to the towered chimneys which should be
> The wind-pipes of good hospitality,
> Through which it breatheth to the open air,
> Betokening life and liberal welfare:
> Lo, there th'unthankful swallow takes her rest,
> And fills the Tunnel with her circled nest.
> Nor half that smoke from all his chimneys goes
> Which one Tobacco pipe drives through his nose:
> (67–74)

The rest of Hall's *Satires* Book V consists of "the greed of landlords," "selfish greed" and "a wastrel heir," in which the satiric targets of "House-keeping's Dead" become clear. The general trend of individualistic life-styles, including the petty housekeeping of landlords, is criticized (McBride 102–03). The satire on the banquet given by a vulgar host is a popular motif in Roman literature, as seen in Horace's *Eighth Satire* and Petronius' *Satyricon*, both of which were probably circulated in Elizabethan England. Among them, Hall's *Virgidemiae* was prohibited by the Bishop's Ban in 1599, as well as other seditious writings (Davenport XXVI; McCabe188–91). This may prove that Hall's satires were highly topical in those days.

In fact, the decline of hospitality was a recurrent motif not only in country house poems, but also in other writings of the early modern period. Robert Greene's pamphlet, *A Quip for an Vpstart Courtier* (1592) refers to the decay of hospitality. It is a fictional dialogue between velvet-breeches and cloth-breeches, or the new gentry and the ancient nobility. The debate is centered on which side has the genuine value. In the epistle dedicated to Thomas Barnabie Esquier, Greene says that "Hospitality was left off, Neighbourhood was exeiled, Conscience was skoft at, and charitie lay frozen in the streets." On the other hand, the patron is admired as "a father of the poore, a supporter of auntient Hospitalitie, an enimie to Pride" (Greene 209–10). As in a series of country house poems, the decline of hospitality is attributed to the pride of the new gentry, and the virtues of the ancient nobility are contrasted with it. Nostalgia for the good old days is also a common motif in country house poems. The following passage retrospectively describes that chimneys of households constantly smoked and the halls were full of guests enjoying communal feasting:

> yes qd. cloth bréeches, he hath this policie, when he maketh a stately place al glorious to the eie and ful of faire chambers and goodlie roomes, and about the house perhaps some threescore Chimnies, yet hée can so cunningly cast by his art, that / thrée of them shal not smoke in the twelue moneths, & so spoiles he much good morter and brick. Why qd. I, the fault is not in the workeman but in the housekeeper, for now a dayes men builde

for to please the eie, and not to profit the poore: they vse no rest but for themselues and their houshold, nor no fire but a little court chimney in their own chamber: how can the poore bricklayer then bée blamed, when the niggardness of the Lord or master is the cause no more chimneys do smoke: for would they vse ancient hospitality as their forefathers did, and value as lightly of pride, as their great grand fathers, then should you sée euery chimney in the house smoke, and prooue that the pore artificer had done his part.

(272)

Chimneys without smoke are recurrently depicted in contemporary writings. In Thomas Dekker's *A Strange Horse-Race* (1613), the readers are addressed: "The Titles of Bookes are like painted Chimnies in great Countrey-houses, make a shew afar off, and catch Trauellers eyes; but comming nere them, neither cast they smoke, nor hath the house the heart to make you drinke" (311–12). In this work, several debates are allegorically presented in a form of horse races. As the author says: "the maine plot of my building is a Moral labyrinth" (312), hospitality is one of the important topics in this work. In the competition between vices and virtues, Blasphemous Insolence runs a race with Innocent Humility, Prodigality competes with Hans-thrift, and finally Niggardliness runs Hospitality. As a result, hospitality is most praised as "the top-bough of all, and the fairest Apple of all," because "hee [Hospitality] kéeps a place in the Countrey, & all the chimnies in it smoke: he spends his money as he spends the water that passeth to his house, it comes thither in great pipes, but it is all consumed in his kichin" (335–36). Again, the satiric targets are the spend-thrift gentry and their pretentious houses. Dekker's intention is clear in his dedicatory epistle: "I must entreat you to blame the vanitie of our times" (309).

The critics have variously interpreted these complaints in relation to a particular social context. L. C. Knights suggests that the decay of hospitality is attributed to the upstart gentry, who acquired their estates by wealth but neglected the noble duty of hospitality (108–17). From a slightly different viewpoint, G. R. Hibbard observes that a series of country house poems thematizes the ethical norm of the pedigreed great houses, which were on the verge of disappearing by the socio-economic transition in pre-capitalist days (159–62). On the other hand, a Marxist historian Raymond Williams claims that the *sponte sua* motif is utilized to veil the realities of a landlord's oppressions like enclosure, severe labor and rack-renting (22–34).

London saw remarkable fluidity of social classes and influx of population throughout the century from Tudor to Stuart (Wrightson 23–31; Heal *Gentry* 7–16). The upper gentry spent more and more time in London or in major towns, and retreated to their country estate just for relaxation and refreshment. It is a common view that communal housekeeping in the countryside decayed because of the new lifestyle of the city-oriented aristocrats (K. Thomas *Man* 246–48; Heal "Idea" 82, 88–89). As Knights and Hibbard discuss, the satiric comments on declining hospitality may partly reflect such a social context. However, as Heal points out, if the lamentation was symptomatically intensified between the 1580s and the late 1630s ("Idea" 80), neither the population shift, nor the fluidity of social classes is a decisive factor of the vogue of the lamentation of the specific period. More importantly, the texts of the early modern satiric writings do not necessarily reflect the exact social realities, because the authors' primary concern is not to write a genuine satire, but to compliment their patrons in order to obtain financial support (Dubrow 153–79; Wayne 77–80; McBride 103–107). This is quite evident in Dekker's statement that the title of his pamphlet is "like a Jesters face, set (howsoever he drawes it) to beget mirth: but his ends are hid to himselfe, and those are to get money" (312). Even in Jonson's "To Penshurst," which is highly artistic, the relationship between patron and client is obvious. Complimenting a real patron by criticizing a fictional third person is a conventional method of patron-client politics, which is often seen in Martial's works (Nauta 188–89).

For another historical document, which is free from patronage consideration, a series of royal proclamations concerning the decay of hospitality may be worth considering. More than ten proclamations were issued between 1596 and 1632, and the gentry was required to go back to their countries and "revive the ancient and laudable custome of this Realme, by house-keeping and hospitality" (Larkin 1: 561). Broadly, three periods of serious enforcement are specified: from 1596 to 1599, from 1614 to 1617 and from 1622 to 1624. Examining the details of the commandments, it becomes clear that the issue of the proclamations was closely related to the growing problem of poverty. Elizabeth urged the local gentry to maintain hospitality in order to relieve the poor in her proclamations of 1596, 1598 and 1599. The enforcement was so strict that a general charge to the assize judges was issued each time, so that the local gentry would not fail to know the order. Moreover, individual delinquents were thoroughly pursued (Heal "Crown" 215–17). The poor problem was nothing particular to the early modern period, but had been a social issue since the Middle Ages. However, the problem went to the extreme in the late Elizabethan period; major Acts of poor relief were quickly established in 1597, 1598 and 1601, all of which became a crucial foundation for the poor-relief legislation of the later period (Jones 22–26; Beier *Problem* 23–29; Slack 122–31; Heal *Hospitality* 131–33).

James also emphasizes the importance of poor-relief in his proclamation of 1615. In time of dearth, further proclamation was issued "for reliefe of the poore, and remedying the high prices of Corne" (1622). However, there was a great difference between Elizabeth and James in the degree of enforcement; there is no evidence of any pursuit of those who offended James' early proclamations (Heal "Crown" 217–21). Moreover, James' commandments are full of nostalgic expressions, praising the virtue of good old communities in the countryside. The following passage is from the 1615 order:

> The decay of Hospitalitie in all the parts of this Our Kingdome, so much the more increaseth, by reason that Noblemen, Knights, and Gentlemen of qualitie, doe rather fall to a more

> private and delicate course of life, after the manner in forreine Countreys, by living in Cities and Townes, [...] to the increase and multiplying of Roagues, Vagabonds and Beggers, and to the breeding of an unreadiness in the Countrey, either for the suppressing of Ryots, tumults and disorders, or for the performing and executing of Our Royal Commandements, upon any suddaine event.
>
> For the redresse of all which inconveniences, We, out of Our Princely care of the common good, do hereby admonish and require all Noblemen, and Gentlemen whatsoever, to live in the steps and examples of their worthy Ancestours, by keeping and entertaining Hospitalitie, and charitable relieving of the poore according to their estate and meanes, not thinking themselves borne for themselves, and their families alone, but for the publique good and comfort of their Countrey, letting them know, that besides their owne well deserving and good fame, and love among the people, it shall be a meanes for them to purchase our good opinion and favour, as the contrary shall not passe without Our note and dislike.
>
> (Larkin 1: 356–57)

James' admiration for hospitality is reminiscent of Jonson's encomia in "To Penshurst," in which the landlord's generosity and the innocent pastoral life are rhetorically idealized. James' liking for idyll is clear because he sometimes visited a country house and even wrote a Horatian elegy entitled: "An Elegy Written by the King concerning his Counsel for ladies and Gentlemen to Depart the City of London according to His Majesty's Proclamation" (Fowler 101–103).

Moreover, James frequently refers to the holiday custom "Christmas" (Heal "Crown" 213–15). In the 1614 order, the gentry are commanded to stay in their country estates "for this whole Winter, or at least during the Christmas time" (Larkin 1: 323). In the following year, a proclamation was issued on 9 December in 1615, just before the Christmas season. In

1616, James made a speech in the Star Chamber and refers to the 1615 proclamation:

> I remember, that before Christmas was Twelue-moneth I made a Proclamation for this cause, That all Gentlemen of qualitie should depart to their owne countreys and houses, to maintaine Hospitalitie amongst their neighbours; which was equiuocally taken by some, as that it was meant onely for that Christmas: But my will and meaning was, and here I declare that my meaning was, that it should always continue.
>
> (McIlwain 343)

Furthermore, the opening statement of the 1632 order is as follows: "the celebration of the feast of Christmasse approacheth, and how needfull it is (especially in this time of scarcity and dearth) to revive the ancient and laudable custome of this Realme, by house-keeping and hospitality" (McIlwain 561). James' appeal for hospitality is strongly associated with the recollection of the old holiday pastime.

James's support for the traditional holiday customs is evident in his *Basilikon Doron* published in 1599, 1603 and 1616, and *A Declaration of Sports* officially published in 1618. Particularly, the latter was a direct defense of old rural festivals, and provoked fierce debates both in his Parliament and the churches, though James tactfully drew a line between acceptable and unacceptable forms of festival in order to avoid the interference with Anglican worship. James' policy was echoed in Charles' proclamation of 1622:

> His Majestie calling to mind, that the celebration of the feast of Christmas now approcheth, which is the fittest time for the exercising of the Charities of the wealthier sort, Hath thought fit, according to the example of His deare Father of blessed memory deceased.
>
> (Larkin 2: 113)

A similar proclamation to revive the old holiday custom was issued in 1627 and 1632, and even *A Declaration of Sports* was reissued in 1633. Reflecting these Stuart contexts, old holiday pastimes in the idyllic past became a popular motif of the poems, masques and stage plays of Jonson and 'the tribe of Ben' such as Robert Herrick and Thomas Carew (Marcus *Politics* 3–6, 106–39; Marcus "Politics" 139–59). Pastoral was also a recurrent motif among 'Spenserian poets' like William Browne, Michael Drayton and George Wither, though they offered rather opposing political perspectives on the royal policy (O'Callaghan 9–10, 46–48). Thus, it seems improbable that the country house poems were completely irrelevant to the Stuart kings' taste (Marcus "Politics" 144–52). In "To Penshurst," Jonson directly refers to the King's sojourn: "King James, when hunting late, this way, /With his brave son, the Prince, they saw thy fires /Shine bright on every hearth" (76–78). The poet may have been interested in enhancing the reputation of the Sidney estate by implying the King's favor to his aristocratic patron (Rathmell 250–60; Evans 120–24). However, considering that a royal pension was awarded to Jonson's 1616 folio, which includes *Epigrams* and *The Forest*, the patron-client politics is also applicable to the relationship between the poet and the King.

Thus, an encomium for the generous landlord does not necessarily mean the actual hospitality, but more or less reflects the patronage consideration of the time. Similarly, satiric comments on illiberality do not exactly represent the real decay of hospitality. Revisionist historians often suggest that the Tudor and Stuart regimes were the great age of English charity in which hospitality was far from decreasing, due to the generosity of wealthy merchants and lower gentry, not of the landed nobility (Jordan 331–32, 338; Pound 69–76). According to Jordan's research (338), the total benefactions from the merchant class are truly notable, although the donors of the class are numerically equal to those of the lower gentry. The rapid increase of monetary value gradually decreased old-style "hospitality," which means giving food and lodging to anyone who comes along. Instead, a different method of material giving, called "charity," replaced it. "Charity" broadly means benevolence to the poor, that is to say, individual alms-giving, public provision for the poor-relief and a bequest or foundation for the benefit of the poor.

According to the *OED*, the early definition of "hospitality" embraced the meaning of general "charity," as the following quotations suggest: "Hospitalitie, that is, herboringe of pore men," and "I can kepe hospitalitye, And geue as much vnto the pore" ('hospitality', n., 1. a). However, "hospitality" and "charity" were gradually differentiated through the early modern period, and the former finally became a synonym of "entertainment," which means inviting someone who is not a stranger: an acquaintance, a neighbor, a friend or kin. This transitional process may be directly relevant to the decay of hospitality and flourish of charity.

It is axiomatic that the charity was far from sufficient in compensating for the decay of hospitality. Severe shortages of food and inflation in the 1590s constantly increased the number of the poor, and the problem of vagrancy was extremely serious. A. L. Beier observes that in reality a very high proportion of vagrants had no lodgings. Even if they could receive food, drink and lodging from the houses of the non-gentry or inns like alehouses, the fee was paid by cash (*Masterless* 79–85, 223). The vagrancy problem was already evident in the mid 16th century. In the 1563 Act, the poor were divided into two categories: deserving and undeserving. The latter was called "idle beggars" or "sturdy beggars" because they wandered from one place to another, seeking a meal and a dole, or more plentiful municipal charity. They were generally identified with dangerous vagabonds and the target of regulation and punishment. It is recorded that a large number of vagabonds flocked to public events like fairs, horse-races, bear-baitings and aristocratic funerals, and the feast was sometimes suppressed due to the disturbance (Clark *Provincial* 221–41; Beier *Masterless* 69–79). In the Act of 1597, the nomination of 'overseers of the poor' was introduced in parishes for the first time, and poor relief became a statutory obligation, though it was a heavy burden for parishes. This reform is significantly relevant to the decay of hospitality. According to the contemporary document, the duty of overseers covered the entire process of poor relief, including practical supervision, taxing contributions, dispensation and so forth (Hindle "Sense" 98–100). Once the responsibility of the poor relief was left to parishes, the distinction between resident and non-resident poor became all the more important. Discriminating between strangers and non-strangers obviously contradicts with the openness of hospitality. Nicholas Breton wrote in "Eleuen of the Clocke" of the day:

> The Dishes set ready for the meat, and the Glasses halfe full of faire water: Now the market people make towards their Horses, and the Beggers begin to draw neere the Townes: the Porrage put off the fire, is set a cooling for the Plough folke, and the great Loafe, and the Cheese are set ready on the Table: [...] The Rich mans Guests are at Courtsey, and I thanke you: and the poore mans Feast is Welcome, and God be with you: [...] the gates be lockt for feare of the Beggers.
>
> (15)

The generous feast is given to anyone who comes, whether one is rich or poor. However, the door is locked for the "beggars," who are probably non-residents.

The several discourses circulated in the Elizabethan and Jacobean periods have made it clear that the nostalgic lamentation of declining hospitality was closely related to the changing socio-economic context. In the country house poems, the comment on hospitality, overtly or covertly reflecting the royal policy, serves as a message to the aristocratic patron whose property heavily depended on the King's favor. As for the pamphlets of Greene and Dekker, the satiric comment on hospitality seems less relevant to the royal policy, but illuminates the fluidity of social classes. This is probably because these works were dedicated to the gentry whose title is "Esquire," not to the nobility. Esquire is the social status which is lower than "Knight" but higher than "Gentleman."

Greene's *Vpstart Courtier* (1592) was reprinted several times, and circulated during the first half of the 17th century. Even after that period, the lamentation of decaying hospitality was recurrent; a pamphlet, *Poor Robins Hue and Cry after Good House-Keeping* (1687) has much in common with *Vpstart Courtier*, complaining that the old-style hospitality of Christmas time declined due to extravagant housekeeping. On the other hand, Tusser's *Husbandry* was reprinted and circulated during the same period. Hospitality was both idealized and lamented in various discourses throughout a century. Printed texts are generally intended for longer-period circulation among the privileged literacy, whereas plays are produced rather rapidly for a wide range of people. Moreover, plays acted in public theaters are markedly differentiated from 'occasional' performances in reception halls of the nobility. In this respect, the degree of political consciousness in the comment on hospitality widely differs between *Summer's Last Will* and *The Winter's Tale*. Moreover, the plays are quite different from other kinds of discourses; they can at once reconstruct a fictional world and the off-stage reality by making use of the art of three-dimensional representation. Thus, the changing connotations of festive representation in the theater may deserve further consideration. In the next chapter, I would like to focus on two Saturnalian plays, which are particularly relevant to the hospitality issue.

II

Late Elizabethan Entertainments

This chapter discusses two short entertainments, *The Old Wives Tale* and *Summer's Last Will and Testament*, which were written around 1590. Both of them can be categorized as Saturnalian plays, containing many topical elements. The dramatic structure is deliberately primitive. One is heavily indebted to folk material, and the other has much in common with pageant and morality plays. First, I would like to focus on *The Old Wives Tale*, which has been considered as one of the most puzzling plays in Elizabethan drama.

1. *The Old Wives Tale*

The front page of the 1595 quarto, the only surviving text, shows that the play was "written by G. P." and "acted by the Queens Maiesties players."[12] It is generally assumed that G. P. stands for George Peele and the work was written between 1588 and 1594. This conjecture is drawn from the evidence that the play includes echoes from Robert Greene's *Orlando Furioso*, in which the Spanish Armada is alluded to. It is also a crucial fact that the Queen's Men were dissolved in 1594 because of financial difficulty (Hook 303–11; Binnie 5–6; Whitworth xviii–xxi).

The text is exceptionally short, consisting of less than 1,000 lines, about half that of a regular play. It has been surmised that the surviving text is a cut version for a provincial performance by a small number of actors (Jenkins 177–85); the play is designed to make double casting easy; soliloquies are frequent and the main story consists of the recovery of stolen identity (McMillin 109–12).[13] The recent study, including the achievement of *REED*, has revealed several facts about the provincial tours (Gurr *Shakespearian* 36–54; Greenfield "Touring" 251–68; Keenan; Holland 45–51), and it is almost certain that the Queen's Men actively performed in provinces as well as in London throughout their career (McMillin 55–67). The possibility of double casting is also proved by the record that the company was divided while touring, probably because it doubled the income. Between 1593 and 1594, when *The Old Wives Tale* was possibly produced, theaters were closed by a privy-council order because of a serious outbreak of the plague. If the Queen's Men acted exclusively in provinces during the time, the surviving text cannot be a cut version but an original one written for a provincial performance. In any case, the play was probably acted more than once at town halls, civic halls, churchyards, county houses, and elsewhere (Keenan 24–143), because the company continued to tour even after 1594 in the provinces such as Coventry, Bath, Leicester, Stratford-upon-Avon and York until 1603. It is also recorded that the Queen's Men played at court on 6th January in 1594, shortly before its dissolution. However, nothing is clear about the performance.

Critics have long discussed the unique structure of *The Old Wives Tale*, which is characterized by a medley of miscellaneous folk motifs. Owing to folkloric researches, the sources have already been well explored (Hook 319–41, 356–76; Binnie 25–29; Whitworth xxiii–xxvii). However, a question remains why the playwright packed several folk motifs into such a short play. They make narrative transitions so abrupt and cause the lack of overall coherence. Some critics attribute them to the playwright's experiment (Marx 117–43). Others pay much attention to originality in the meta-theatrical device blurring the distinction between the storytelling framework and the dramatic action (Free 53–61). However, the majority of the cases overlook the possibility that the play was designed for a provincial performance, not for a commercial theater in London. Jackson I. Cope observes that the play is full of Saturnalian rituals representing death and rebirth in his "Peele's Old Wives Tale: Folk Stuff into Ritual Form." Cope puts forward a question:

> to whom was the folk material directed in *The Old Wives Tale?* A University and Court dramatist, Peele did not write for the "folk". Yet this play was quite possibly a provincial touring text. And quite possibly not. [...] There was no audience but the author and posterity.
>
> (327)

Since the Queen's Men performed in provinces as well as in London, as the recent study suggests, the folk material seems quite appropriate for the country audiences. However, the question of the dramatic structure is still to be resolved.

John D. Cox gives a significant comment in his "Homely Matter and Multiple Plots": "*The Old Wives Tale* has been compared to the kind of rustic production that Shakespeare gently parodies in the tragical mirth of Pyramus and Thisbe" (344). Cox does not compare the two "rustic" entertainments. He, however, observes that *The Old Wives Tale* has something in common with "Pyramus and Thisby," which is a clumsy household entertainment acted by craftsmen in *A Midsummer Night's Dream*.

Critics have variously discussed the dramatic function of the play-within-a play in *A Midsummer Night's Dream*. New Historicists observe that the final dissolution of the 'play' into the outermost framework of Theseus' wedding banquet represents the social tension between the craftsmen's low culture and the aristocratic high culture (Patterson 52–70; P. Williams 55–66; Montrose 68–86). From a meta-theatrical viewpoint, some critics regard the play-within-a play as a parody, in which the craftsmen's performance is contrasted with the professional acting. In other words, the awkwardness of 'the play' contrasts with the sophistication of the play. For example, Clifford Davidson discusses the craftsmen's play-within-a play in connection with the trading companies of Coventry, which Shakespeare probably witnessed in his childhood (88–89). According to Davidson, "beards, wigs and masks," referred to by the actors of "Pyramus and Thisby," were the essential costumes of the Coventry plays or other civic plays of the Middle Ages (92–94).[14] Wearing masks and other ornaments is also a common device in Mumming, which is the origin of Disguisings and Masques (Wickham 136–37). Davidson draws the conclusion that the craftsmen's performance "serves by its burlesque of amateur actors to set apart their play-within-a play from the main actions of *A Midsummer Night's Dream* and hence to provide a comment on the role of imagination in the theater itself — a theater which Shakespeare's company represented at its professional best" (95; See also Robinson 192–205). Davidson's argument focuses on the different quality of acting between the amateur and the professional. However, the play-within-a play may be too lengthy to be a simple parody. Moreover, this is the final scene of the multi-layered festive drama. Considering that the entire action of *A Midsummer Night's Dream* comes from ridiculous inversions of the May festival, the clumsy 'play' may have much deeper implication.

The festive mood is predominant in the craftsmen's acting scene. When Bottom performs the death of Pyramus, he awkwardly cries, "Now die, die, die, die, die" (5.1.306). The 'audiences' harshly comment on this.

> *Dem.* No die, but an ace, for him; for he is but one.
> *Lys.* Less than an ace, man; for he is dead, he is nothing.
> *The.* With the help of a surgeon he might yet recover, and yet prove an ass.
> (5.1.307–11)

Theseus tells a joke: "a surgeon" could revive the dead Pyramus. The original audiences must have noticed that he refers to the old ritual play of St. George. In the surviving texts of the St. George plays, there are variants of the plot. However, it is a common ritual that a comic hero fights for wooing, revived by a doctor several times. The game ends happily with the attainment of love (Tiddy 141–257; Baskervill "Mummers'" 241–50; Gassner 30–32; Chambers *English*: 42–46; Helm 11–16). The repetition of death and rebirth symbolizes the life cycles of vegetation, and the play was customarily acted in celebration of the harvest and weddings (Chambers *Mediaeval* 1: 226; James 272–78; Laroque *Shakespeare's* 110–11).

Theseus' allusion to "a surgeon" is nothing but a joke. However it surely illuminates the wrong combination of the classical tragedy "Pyramus and Thisby" and the fool-like actors reminiscent of the St. George play. The mismatch is restated by Theseus who requests that their performance should end with "a Bergomask dance" instead of the epilogue. The allusions to these primitive folk entertainments may not necessarily mock the amateur acting, but make the audience aware that the on-going situation is thoroughly ridiculous, mingling highbrow and lowbrow, seriousness with the comic. When Theseus asks the master of the revels, "what masques, what dances / shall we have?" (5.1.32–33), he does not seem to expect such a ridiculous entertainment. However, the oxymoronic title attracts him: "Merry and tragical? Tedious and brief? / That is hot ice and wondrous strange snow. / How shall we find the concord of this discord?" (5.1.58–60) Theseus' comments suggest that the play-within-a play works as a festive fantasy, in which two opposite ends temporarily meet and become one. This may be quite an appropriate Saturnalian entertainment to end 'a midsummer night's dream.'

The mismatch is also recognized in the combination of the actors and 'the stage.' According to recent research, household entertainment sponsored by the aristocracy continued throughout the age of Shakespeare. However, the household theater, or the "patron theater," was a place to demonstrate the aesthetic and intellectual sophistication of the patron

(Westfall 266–80). It is therefore a totally ironic setting that the craftsmen act a play in an aristocratic household. Quoting Samuel Cox's letter to Sir Christopher Hatton, written in 1591, Thomas Pettitt illustrates the different types of local drama of the time (464). In the letter, Cox laments the popularity of commercialized theater and recollects the past when plays were acted exclusively in households and parish communities. Cox divides the players into three. The first group is "such as were in wages with the king." The second group consists of household players:

> The second sort were such as pertained to noblemen, and were ordinary servants in their house, and only for Christmas times used such plays, without making profession to be players to go abroad for gain[...]
> (Chambers 4: 237)

The third group includes craftsmen:

> The third sort were certain artisans in good towns and great parishes, as shoemakers, tailors, and such like, that used to play either in their town-halls, or some time in churches, to make the people merry; where it was lawful for all persons to come without exacting any money for their access, having only somewhat gathered of the richer sort by the churchwardens for their apparel and other necessaries.
> (Chambers 4: 237)

It is worth noting that Cox differentiates household players from "artisans," such as "shoemakers" and "tailors," who play in "their town-halls" or "churches." Cox also suggests that these players entertain "all persons to come" and "make people merry." Probably the plays of St. George and Robin Hood belonged to this category. It is also noted that the artisans acted a play for charitable purposes. "Other necessaries" probably mean the fund for fabric of parish churches and aids for the poor in the communities (Wickham 146–48; Weimann 27). In fact, one of the surviving texts of the St. George plays includes the stage direction for collecting money from the audience:

> FATHER CHRISTMAS. So, ladies and gentlemen, your sport has now ended.
> Therefore, behold this box, which is highly commended!
> The box it would speak, if it had but a tongue,
> Come throw in your money and think it no wrong.
> (FATHER CHRISTMAS starts collecting money in his box.)
> (Gassner 32)

In *A Midsummer Night's Dream*, a craftsman says that Duke will give Bottom "sixpence a day during his life" (4.2.22), if the play is successfully acted. The fictional setting of the play-within-a play is doubly ridiculous, mismatching the players and the play, and the players and the stage.

John D. Cox suggests that *The Old Wives Tale* has something in common with the "rustic" production of "Pyramus and Thisby." Moreover, *The Old Wives Tale* is a real household entertainment acted by a professional company. The clumsy structure of the play may have much more implication. First, the story-telling framework is worth special attention. The old wife, Madge tells a story for entertaining the guests, who have lost their way and asked for lodgings for the night. One of the guests says, "me thinkes, Gammer, / a merry winters tale would drive away the time trimly" (82–83). For the present audience, this is the only clue to knowing the specific time of the story-telling framework: this is winter. However, several hints are scattered in the text, implying that 'the story' is particularly designed for a Christmas entertainment, which the original audience may have recognized.

The first clue is in Madge's humble banquet. She extends good hospitality to the strangers who come from "Towne":

> *Old Woman.* Welcom Clunch and good fellowes al that

>   come with my good man, for my good mans sake,
>   come on, sit downe, here is a peece of cheese and a pudding
>   of my owne making.
> *Ant.* Thanks Gammer a good example for the wives of our
>   towne.
> *Frol.* Gammer thou and thy good man sit lovingly together,
>   we come to chat and not to eate.
> *Smith.* Well Masters if you will eate nothing take away:
>   Come, what doo we to passe away the time? Lay a crab in
>   the fire to rost for Lambes-wooll; what, shall wee have a
>   game at Trumpe or Ruffe to drive away the time, how say
>   you?
>
>   (56–68)

Among several dishes mentioned above, "Lambes-wooll" is particularly worth noting. According to the *OED*, lamb's wool is defined as "a drink consisting of hot ale mixed with the pulp of roasted apples, and sugared and spiced" ('lamb's wool', n., 2). The ale with roasted apples frequently appears in the rural scenes of contemporary works. In the last song of *Love's Labor's Lost*, Winter sings, "roasted crabs hiss in the bowl" (5.2.925). In *A Midsummer Night's Dream*, Puck talks about his mischief: "sometime lurk I in a gossip's bowl, / In very likeness of a roasted crab, / And when she drinks, against her lips I bob, / And on her withered dewlop pour the ale" (2.1.47–50). The most succinct description is found in *The Cobler of Caunterburie* (1590). The anonymous author says in his epistle to the readers, this work is a parody of Chaucer's *The Canterbury Tales* and only written for a pastime to be read "when the Farmer is set in his Chaire turning (in a winters euening) the crabbe in the fier" (Creigh 20). Looking at these examples, the ale with roasted crab apples was probably a popular homemade drink of the winter season. However, in none of these quotations above, it is called "lamb's wool."

Robert Herrick's "Twelfe Night, or King and Queene" gives some useful information about the lamb's wool. The poem is included in his

Hesperides published in 1648. Standing on his royalist viewpoint, the volume includes several poems about old folk festivals such as May-poles, Hock-carts, Christmas and Wakes. In Herrick's "Twelfe Night," "lamb's wool" was specifically related to the wassail on Twelfth Night:

> Now, now the mirth comes
> With the cake full of plums,
> Where Beane's the *King* of the sport here;
> Beside we must know,
> The Pea also
> Must revell, as *Queene*, in the Court here.
>
> [...]
>
> Next crowne the bowle full
> With gentle lambs-wooll;
> Adde sugar, nutmeg and ginger,
> With store of ale too;
> And thus ye must doe
> To make the wassaile a swinger.
>
> Give then to the King
> And Queene wassailing:
> And though with ale ye be whet here;
> Yet part ye from hence,
> As free from offence,
> As when ye innocent met here.
>   (1–30)

The *OED* defines wassail as "a custom formerly observed on Twelfth-night and New-Year's Eve of drinking healths from the wassail-bowl"('wassail', n., 3). In Herrick's poem, this drink is called "lamb's wool." Even today, "wassail" is a familiar word sung in Christmas carols.[15] "Lamb's wool" is also alive as a traditional drink served on various festive occasions (Hazlitt *Faiths* 358–59), especially for the feast of Epiphany, namely Twelfth Night.

My purpose is not to specify the time setting of Peele's old wife's tale, but to suggest that the original audiences associated the play with the Christmas festivity. In the very beginning of the play, three travelers enter and tell the audience that they have lost their way in the wood. However, they are in the merriment of the festivity, singing "Three merry men," which is also sung by Sir Toby in *Twelfth Night*. Furthermore, in the banquet scene quoted above, Madge's hospitality is praised as "a good example for the wives of our [their] / towne" (60–61). Another guest also says, "This Smith leads a life as merrie as a King with / Madge his wife" (69–70). They talk about the hospitality at Christmas, which is a dying custom in towns and cities.

The issue of hospitality resonates in the whole action of the drama. As mentioned above, the play consists of a medley of folk tales, and the narrative transitions are so abrupt that it is difficult to find the overall coherence. However, all of the motifs are more or less related to the issue of charity, into which the play may be integrated. Among many critics, Howard C. Cole (544–50), Steven C. Young (64–76) and Binnie (45 n. 152, 47 n. 209, 55 n. 344) note this point, though very briefly.

The first motif is about the two brothers who are seeking their abducted sister, Delya. When they arrive at the "chalklie Cliffs of Albion," they meet a poor old man, Erestus who sits at the crossroad and is gathering "hips and hawes, and stickes and strawes" for food. The first charity is "almes pennie" from the brothers to Erestus:

> 2 *Bro.* Father, here is an Almes pennie for mee, and if I
>   speede in that I goe for, I will give thee as good a Gowne of
>   gray as ever thou diddest weare.
> 1 *Bro.* And Father here is another almes pennie for me, and
>   if I speede in my journey, I will give thee a Palmers staffe
>   of yvorie, and a scallop shell of beaten gold.
>   (148–53)

According to Binnie, this is "the second gesture of spontaneous giving, the first being Clunch's and Madge's hospitality" (45 n. 152). However, the alms-giving is essentially different from the old-style hospitality extended by Clunch and Madge. The brothers say that the alms penny is "for me," not for the sake of the old man. They promise to further reward him with a "Gowne of gray" and "Palmers staffe of yvorie," if his spell really helps them. This is not one-way giving but a kind of give-and-take. Erestus, an enchanted old man, is a touchstone of the charitable mind, receiving alms and telling the fortune of every person who enters the stage. The riddles told by him are designed to create the central plot of the play, based on the folk tales "The Three Heads of the Well" and "The Grateful Dead" (Jacobs 218–22; Gerould 71–75)[16]. Both of the tales give the moral that charitable conducts make a fortune.

The second motif is a tale of misery told by Lampriscus to Erestus. In their dialogue, "neighbourhood" and "brotherhood" are frequently mentioned, and the importance of reciprocity is stressed (Cole 548):

> *Lam.* Neighbour on nothing, but on the matter I so often mooved to you: if you do anything for charity, helpe me; if for neighborhood or brotherhood, helpe me: never was one so combered as is poore Lampriscus: and to begin, I pray receive this potte of Honny to mend you fare.
> *Old Man.* Thankes neighbor, set it downe, Honny is alwaies welcome to the Beare. And now neighbour let me heere the cause of your coming.
>
> (203–10)

In Elizabethan parishes, helping a neighbor was particularly respected as a way of poor relief. Consequently, the known poor and poor strangers were strictly differentiated (Heal "Idea" 75–77; Heal *Hospitality* 387–88). Madge states that Lampriscus is "a beggar, and dwelt upon a greene" (247). It is highly satirical that Lampriscus and Erestus, who are the 'beggars,' overstate the importance of the mutual help in the community.

In the third motif, the most caricatured character, Huanebango appears with his two-handed swords, attended by Booby. He is a stock figure of the braggart who speaks in hexameter like the soldier in Plautus' *The Braggart Warrior*. In this play, he is the only person who refuses alms-giving, saying that "Huanebango giveth no Cakes for Almes, aske of / them that give giftes for poore Beggars" (314–15). On the other hand, Booby mercifully gives Erestus a piece of cake, and complains of his master's pedantic musings about charity:

> [...] whoo he comes uppon me with a
> superfantiall substance, and the foyson of the earth, that I
> know not what he meanes: If hee came to me thus, and
> said, my friend Booby or so, why I could spare him a peece
> with all my heart; but when he tells me how God hath en-
> riched mee above other fellows with a Cake: why hee
> makes me blinde and deafe at once.
>
> (321–27)

It is satirical that Huanebango connects a piece of cake with God's favor. As seen in the *Book of Homilies*, the virtue of alms-deeds was often preached to the ordinary parishioners in a very plain manner. As a result, the religious spirit of charity was reduced to a simple idea of rewarding: how much God extends his favor and what fruits and commodities will come in return (Harrison 22–30). The practical idea of charity as well as the pedantic theory seems to be satirized in the third motif.

The last motif is about Eumenides' charitable contribution to the burial of poor Jack. His charitable conduct comes from Erestus' riddle that "Bestowe thy almes, give more than all, / Till dead mens bones come at thy call" (445–46). Eumenides' charity serves to integrate the entangled situations into one happy ending, satirically reflecting the reality of the parish church. For example, the churchwarden and sexton appear and claim that they cannot afford to pay for the poor who have no money for their burial. This situation is not completely fictional. According to

Churchwardens' accounts, burial fees and mortuaries were sometimes unpaid by the poor (Harrison 70–73). Sexton says, "pay me my fees, and let the / rest runne on in the quarters accounts, and put it downe for / one of your good deedes a Gods name" (461–63). This is another satirical comment on charity. His complaint further continues: "we may pull downe the steeple, sell the Belles, / and thatche the chauncell" (493–94). Charitable conducts are far from rewarding, as the church is in poverty. One of Jack's friends says, "will you not when he is dead let him have Christmas buriall?" (467–68) The editors of the play assume that "Christ- / mas buriall" is a malapropism of "Christian buriall" (Hook 433 n.467; Binnie 64 n.488; Whitworth 27 n.452). However, "Christmas," an occasion of charity, may be interpreted as a metonymy of "charitable," just as "Christmas feast" means a feast for the poor. Thus the play, 'the old wife's tale at Christmas night,' is an integrated story of charity.

As I have discussed in the previous chapter, the correlation between charity and Christmas derives from the old custom of the Saturnalia, in which the distinction between the rich/master and the poor/servants was temporarily suspended, commemorating Saturnus, the agricultural god in the Golden Age. In Peele's *The Old Wives Tale*, the imagery of harvest is abundant, as Jackson Cope suggests. First, the songs of sowing and reaping are inserted twice, though they are not relevant to the development of the plot. Secondly, a Head comes up with "eares of Corne" from the well, and again appears "full of golde." This unmistakably echoes the abundant provisions of the Golden Age. Thirdly, Erestus, who is "seeming an olde and miserable man: / And yet I am [he is] in Aprill of my [his] age" (196–97), finally has his youthful appearance restored, which had been stolen by the sorcerer Sacrapant. On the contrary, Sacrapant who "seemth yong and pleasant to behold, / And yet is aged, crooked, weake and numbe" (348–49) recovers his shape of the old conjurer. This was probably acted by doubling, and effectively symbolized an agricultural life cycle: death/rebirth (McMillin 110).

The Saturnalian element is also found in old festive drama, as Roger Renwick illustrates the parallels between *The Old Wives Tale* and mummer's plays in detail (433–55). Above all, Huanebango's wooing action overlaps with the comic ritual of the St. George play, and his two-handed swords remind giants and other performers in Midsummer Shows (Binnie 51). Booby refers to the novelty of his own costume: "Harke you sir, harke you; First know I have / here the flurting feather, and have given the Parish the / start for the long stocke:" (272–74). This is a puzzling line and different readings have been offered. Binnie says that Booby's clothes are probably outmoded, because he is the Clown of Huanebango, a parody of the Knight Errant. If Huanebango's two-handed swords are the properties of the old folk play, Booby's feather and boots were likely to be the old-fashioned playing costumes.[17]

It is a kind of meta-theatrical device that the characters themselves comment on the ongoing performance. For example, in *A Midsummer Night's Dream*, the craftsmen talk about wearing "masks" and imply that their 'play' will be anachronistic. In the acting scene, Theseus mocks their clumsy performance, alluding to the "surgeon" of the St. George play and "a Bergomask dance." In *A Midsummer Night's Dream*, such a meta-theatrical device is only applied in the play-within-a play. On the other hand, in *The Old Wives Tale*, the meta-theatricality extends to the entire action of the drama. First, Madge's narration is interrupted by the actors who "come to tell your [her] tale for you [her]." In some transitions of the motifs, the narrators comment on the action, but they are immediately interrupted by the next actor's entrance led by the cue: "soft, who comes here?" It has been the most mysterious point that the narrators can cross the boundary between the framework and the action without any difficulty.

In this respect, Mary G. Free gives a significant analysis of the meta-theatrical function in *The Old Wives Tale*. She notes that the structure of the play is characteristic of the Tudor Interludes, maintaining a sense of contact with the audience at a great hall (55). Direct address to the audience is one of the key interlude techniques (J. Hill 76–108). Free observes that Madge's story-telling works on two levels: her audience on the stage and the audience external, namely the two pages and the assembled guests of the household. Free attributes the ambiguous distinction between the framework and the action to the necessity of controlling these two kinds of audiences. Free's argument is quite persuasive, based on the fundamental concept of the household entertainment. However, one of the pages comments on the play, "Why this goes rounde without a fiddling stick"(243). He compares Madge's tale to a country dance to a fiddler's tune, as if he is mocking the defective structure of the play. This may hint that the play borrows the structure of the primitive folk drama rather than of the Tudor interludes.

Before theater was commercialized, almost all drama was festive, because the theatrical representation was merely one component of the festive entertainments. The play had no scenario, rather improvised and untrimmed. According to Twycross, there were potentially three groups involved in the festivity: "active players, passive players and spectators" (1–9). For example, in the St. George play, Father Christmas is a kind of "passive player" because each entrance of the actors is led by his cue: "Come in!" and "Clear the way" (Gassner 30). He can also directly address the spectators. Similarly in the Robin Hood play, Robin himself introduces each play as a presenter (J. Manley 279–88). In other words, Father Christmas and Robin cross the boundary between the fictional world and reality just like Madge and the pages in *The Old Wives Tale* do.

However, it is clear that *The Old Wives Tale* is not a simple parody of the old folk drama; the play was probably acted at a "patron theater" in a province around 1590. The performance may have required intellectual sophistication shared with the audience. In this respect, the burlesque elements of the play take on further significance. Some critics regard *The Old Wives Tale* as a parody of contemporary romantic plays, stuffed with the characteristics of whole genre of romance (Doebler 412–21; Rockey 268–75). However, the structure like "a country dance to a fiddler's tune" is not necessarily a parody of any genre, but may be the original genre. The play consists of a series of seemingly irrelevant tales told by different persons and in different meters. This is characteristic of Menippean satire, which was undoubtedly popular among the Renaissance writers (Suzuki 55–97).

In 1595, shortly after *The Old Wives Tale* was produced, *A Pleasaunt Satyre or Poesie: Wherein is Discouered the Catholicon of Spayne, and the Chiefe Leaders of the League* was published. This is the first English translation from Jean Le Roy's *La Satyre Ménippée* (1594), a satirical writing against Jesuits. At the end of the English edition, "The French Printers Discovuse, Tovching the Exposition of these Words, Higuirero of hell, and concerning other matters, which he learned of the Author himselfe" is added, and "Satyre Menippized" is defined as follows:

> [...]this word Satyre, doth not only signifie a poesie, containing euill speech in it, for the reproofe, either of publike vices, or of particular faults of some certaine persons, of which sort are those of Lucilius, Horace, Iuuenal, and Persius: but also all sortes of writinges, replenished with sundry matters, and diuers argumentes, hauing prose and verse intermixed or mingled therewithall, as if it were powdered neats tongues interlarded. [...] In olde time, some made them to rehearse their injurious verses all alone, without any other matter in them, then railing and speaking euill of eueryone, afterwards men mingled them with Comedie players, who brought them into their acts, to make the people laugh: at the last, the more graue and serious Romanes chased them altogether out of their Theaters, and receiued in their place, Vices in playes: but the more wise and wittie Poets vsed them, to content therewithal, their owne bad spirit of euill speaking, which some of them thought to bee the chiefe goodness.
>
> (*Pleasant* 202–203)

Different from Horacian satire, Menippean satire is "sundry matters, and diuers argumentes, hauing prose and verse intermixed or mingled." Peele's play rightly consists of the medley/*satura* of seemingly miscellaneous matters told in different meters. The publication date of this pamphlet suggests that Peele did not read this passage before the production of *The Old Wives Tale*. However, Peele was undoubtedly familiar with the Menippean satirists like Lucian, Apuleius and Petronius, all of whom are mentioned in the pamphlet above (203).

The Golden Ass written by either Apuleius or Lucian has been commonly regarded as one of the possible sources of *The Old Wives Tale* (Hook 337–38). Petronius' *Satyricon* may be more relevant to the play, since the Saturnalian elements are predominant in Petronius' work (Suzuki 30–34). Temporal equality between master and servant is a typical Saturnalian motif. In *The Old Wives Tale*, this is obvious in the relationship between Eumenides and the ghost Jack. Jack says to Eumenides, "Ile serve you," but Eumenides answers "I am / content to entertaine thee, not as a servant, but a copartner / in my journey" (720–22). Then Eumenides promises to give Jack half of everything that he gets on his journey. As a result, Jack demands Eumenides to "have halfe" of his lady:

> *Eumen.* Well ere I will falsifie my worde unto my friend,
>   take her all, heere Jack ile give her thee.
> *Jack.* Nay neither more nor lesse Maister, but even just
>   halfe.
> *Eumen.* Before I will falsifie my faith unto my
>   friend, I will divide hir, Jacke thou shalt have halfe.
>   (893–98)

This is nothing more than a Saturnalian joke. However, a similar episode is present in *Satyricon*:

> [...] "As you have wickedly broken our agreement and the friendship between us, collect your things at once, and find some other place to corrupt."
>
> He did not resist, but after we had divided our spoils with scrupulous honesty he said, "And now we must divide the boy

too." I thought this was a parting joke. But he drew his sword murderously, and said, "You shall not enjoy this treasure that you brood over all alone. I am rejected, but I must carve off my share too, even with this sword."

(Petronius p. 185–87)

As the author of *A Pleasaunt Satyre or Poesie* says, Menippean satire is a literary form of "all sortes of writings," not of the drama. However, some of the contemporary writings show that the story-telling is a very appropriate form of gathering sundry matters. For example, medieval jest books and *The Canterbury Tales* have a medley of inset stories told by different narrators. They were certainly popular throughout the Elizabethan period, as seen in the publication of *The Cobbler of Caunterburie* (1590), which is a parody of *The Canterbury Tales*. *The Cobbler* consists of six inset stories told by different narrators, in verse and prose. The stories are seemingly irrelevant to each other. However, five out of six episodes are relevant to the cuckoldry of the clergy, and so anti-cleric satire is obvious. A similar device is in a Spanish picaresque story, *The Life of Lazarillo de Tormes*, which was translated into English in 1586. Though the stories are told by the same narrator, five out of nine masters satirized in the inset stories are the clergy.

The Old Wives Tale seemingly comprises irrelevant folkloric tales, but they are skillfully integrated by the social satire on charity. The story-telling structure deriving from Menippean satire/*satura*, which is hardly intelligible to us, may have been easily recognized by the contemporary sophisticated audience. As there is no information about the first performance of *The Old Wives Tale*, it is uncertain whether the play was really successful or not. Yet, it is possible to say that the novelty of this jumbled Saturnalian entertainment may have satisfied the sophisticated patron of the day.

2. Summer's Last Will and Testament

Thomas Nashe's *Summer's Last Will and Testament* was written for an occasional performance at Archbishop Whitgift's household in Croydon at the end of the summer of 1592, when the outbreak of the plague was serious in London. At that time, Nashe was under the patronage of Whitgift, because he was one of the pamphleteers who were employed by the ecclesiastical side to write against Martin in a series of Marprelate controversies. The original audience of the play was probably learned men and scholars who were invited to Whitgift's house. It is important that the play was written for a particular audience at a particular time and place (Hibbard *Thomas* 90).

The play is similar to a pageant, as Will Summer, "a Chorus," says in the prologue: "'tis no Play neyther, but a shewe" (75). Songs and dances are presented several times by the actors who are dressed in their allegorical costumes. The dramatic personas represent four seasons, seasonal festivals and mythological figures. The fictional setting of the play symbolically overlaps with the off-stage reality: a serious outbreak of the plague is threatening people's life at the end of the summer. The central figure of the play is Summer, who is dying from the plague and intends to make his last will and testament. He summons his possible heirs one by one and makes them account for all the money spent, so that he may find the best keeper of his bequest. As a result, Autumn inherits Summer's property, and Winter becomes his overseer. Although the plot is simple, the account given by each character has deep implication.

Besides the pageant-like elements, the play has much in common with the morality plays. C. L. Barber's analysis of the play in his *Shakespeare's Festive Comedy* suggests that the play is "reminiscent of mediaeval *debats* and of the encounters between gay vices and sober virtues in the morality plays" (60). Barber divides the dramatic personas into three groups. First, Ver, Harvest and Bacchus are "the most vital spokesmen for everybody's pastimes" and speak in prose. Secondly, pageant-like characters such as Vertumnus, Sol and Orion speak in verse. Finally, Christmas and Backwinter are categorized as kill-joy characters (59–60). Barber, who finds dichotomy between the first and the third group, says that the debate is "primarily shaped by a holiday-everyday opposition" (60). Barber's view mainly comes from the last scene, in which Summer rebukes Christmas' stinginess with money for his own festivity. Summer says, "Amend thy maners, breathe thy rusty gold: / Bounty will win thee loue, when thou art old" (1731–32). Summer's didactic speech is surely reminiscent of the triumph of virtues in the morality plays. Barber concludes that the play was written as a defense of the "holiday spirit," which was under persistent attack by the Puritans. Barber's view is still influential.[18] Marie Axton's political analysis in her "*Summer's Last Will and Testament*: Revels' End" stands on Barber's. She notes that the play's text was published in 1600, shortly before James' accession, and reads the fears that revels might come to an end in anticipation of the new monarch who comes from Scotland, where the Christmas festivity was already prohibited.

It is true that the Christmas' anti-festive attitude is remarkable. However, the overall plot is concerned with the accounts given by the festive characters, not with the festivity itself. The characters often refer to "thrift or spendthrift" and "liberality or illiberality." The festival may be simply a vehicle for representing a much larger social issue. This assumption is reinforced by the final scene, when Christmas is compared to a "god of hospitality." Summer states that Christmas belongs to "nobility." Will Summer also comments that "he was a Caualiere and good fellow" (1543).

> *Summer.* Christmas, I tell thee plaine, thou art a snudge,
> And wert not that we loue thy father well,
> Thou shouldst haue felt what longs to Auarice.
> It is the honor of Nobility
> To keepe high dayes and solemne festiuals:
> Then, to set their magnificence to view,
> To frolick open with their fauorites,
> And vse their neighbours with all curtesie;
> When thou in huggar mugger spend'st thy wealth.

(1722–30)

In a series of country house poems, as mentioned in the previous chapter, liberality of the landed nobility was highly praised and idealized, and their illiberality was the target of harsh satires. Since hospitality was one of the public concerns in the late Elizabethan and early Stuart periods, the clergy and the bishops were particularly responsible for the care of the community (Heal *Prelates* 237–64; Heal "Archbishops" 544–63). Considering that the play was patronized by Archbishop Whitgift, who was directly involved in the hospitality issue, Summer's didactic speech quoted above has much topicality.

If the play was prepared for the highly sophisticated audience invited to Whitgift's palace, it was probably designed as an intellectual social satire, rather than a simple show or a morality entertainment. Sherri Geller significantly refers to the play as "the sophisticated comedy or satire," in which "satire participates in the gallimaufry and produces dramatic continuity" (151), though her discussion is confined to Nashe's satire on his illiberal patron, Archbishop Whitgift.

The playwright's satiric intention is also evident in Will Summer's dramatic function. He freely comes in and out of the action, just like the narrators of *The Old Wives Tale*. He introduces his role as follows:

> Ile sit as a Chorus, and flowte the Actors and
> him at the end of euery Sceane: I know they will not
> interrupt me, for feare of marring of all: but looke to your
> cues, my masters; for I intend to play the knaue in cue,
> and put you besides all your parts, if you take not the
> better heede. Actors, you Rogues, come away, cleare your
> throats, blowe your noses, and wype your mouthes ere you
> enter, that you may take no occasion to spit or to cough,
> when you are non plus.
>
> (91–99)

He not only comments on the play, but directly addresses the players like Old Father Christmas of the St. George play, all the while keeping his distance from both the players and the playwright. After he saw Solstitium's boring performance, he mocks the clumsiness of the play:

> *Will Summer.* Fye, fye, of honesty, fye: Solstitium is an asse, perdy; this play is a gally-maufrey: fetch mee some drinke, some body. What cheere, what cheere, my hearts? are not you thirsty with listening to this dry sport?
> (421–24)

Will Summer goes so far as to say that Nashe is "the person of the Idiot our Playmaker" (21–22). This probably comes from the playwright's consideration that Will Summer's satirical comments camouflage more dangerous satires included in the play. Moreover, his name is identical with that of Henry VIII's famous jester. This may also camouflage his outspokenness under the name of the famous court fool.

The accounts are made by six characters, Ver, Solstitium, Sol, Orion, Harvest, and Bacchus. Each account represents one's own social status and serves to epitomize contemporary society. The first reporter is Ver, who is a "monstrous unthrift." His account is interrupted by Morris dances. He praises beggary, as Will Summer says, "So we come hither to laugh and be merry, and / we heare a filthy beggerly Oration in the prayse of beggery" (346–47). He is regarded as a representative of the poor, who have no estates and no fortune. The second account is given by Solstitium, who loves "to dwell betwixt the hilles and dales; / Neyther to be so great to be enuide, / Nor yet so poore the world should pitie me" (378–80). He represents the moderation of the middle-class. The third reporter is Sol, who enters "very richly attired." Autumn criticizes him:

> *Autumne.* O arrogance exceeding all beliefe!
> Summer my lord, this sawcie vpstart Iacke,
> That now doth rule the chariot of the Sunne,

> And makes all starres deriue their light from him,
> Is a most base insinuating slaue,
> The sonne of parsimony and disdain.
>
> (471–76)

He represents the "upstart" gentry, who were frequently satirized in the contemporary writings, as in Robert Greene's *A Quip for an Vpstart Courtier*. The next reporter is Orion. He is a hunter called "the dogstar," and speaks about dogs "in their defense." 'The dog' is obviously associated with the philosophy of the Cynic school. Orion also refers to the Stoic school. Both schools respect austerity and asceticism. Thus Orion's stoicism is contrasted with Ver's encomium for beggary.

One of the most important accounts is made by Harvest, who is a "goodman" and "yeoman." He enters with a scythe on his neck, convivially singing a traditional hock-cart song. He is surprisingly industrious, and the public calls him "an ingrosser of the common store." Harvest denies the accusation, and makes an eloquent defense of his hospitality:

> I keepe good hospitality for hennes & geese: Gleaners
> are oppressed with heauy burdens of my bounty:
> They rake me, and eate me to the very bones,
> Till there be nothing left but grauell and stones,
> and yet I give no almes, but deuoure all? They say, when
> a man cannot heare well, you heare with your haruest eares:
> but if you heard with your haruest eares, that is, with the
> eares of corne which my almes-cart scatters, they would
> tell you that I am the vey poore mans boxe of pitie,
> that there are more holes of liberality open in haruests
> heart then in a siue, or a dust-boxe.
>
> (873–83)

In the sixteenth century, yeoman, who belonged to the wealthier social class, were still demanded to entertain their poor husbandmen, but the reality was different because the moral and social values gradually changed. Praise for the good hospitality of the yeoman class and the anxiety over their continued ability to entertain the poor were frequently addressed in contemporary writings (Heal *Hospitality* 377–88). Harvest's speech quoted above, partly overstated and rhetorical, rightly reflects the social context. Summer's praise for Harvest is comically out of point. Summer says, "Rest from thy labours till the yeere renues, / And let the husbandmen sing of thy prayse" (922–23). However, the farm work is distributed over the year. After the busiest harvest time, from August to September, farmers have to prepare for the large fairs in order to sell and buy their stock. In early December, plough land is prepared for beans, and further preparations for winter are made (Campbell 209–10). Harvest's response is satirical:

> Rest from my labours, and let the husband-
> men sing of my prayse? Nay, we doe not meane to rest
> so; by your leaue, we'le haue a largesse amongst you, e're
> we part.
>
> (924–27)

Harvest's demand for largesse is one of the playwright's devices to compliment his patron. Harvest says:

> [...] I see
> charitie waxeth cold, and I thinke this house be her habi-
> tatiō, for it is not very hot.
>
> (931–33)

"This house" clearly refers to Whitgift's household. Then Harvest praises Whitgift's good hospitality, and says that his house is "not very hot," stressing that it is, literally or metaphorically, opened to the public (Hibbard *Thomas* 88–89; Hutson 167–70). One of the contemporary biographers, George Paul actually refers to Whitgift's hospitality in his

The Life of John Whitgift:

> He had a desire always to keep a great and bountiful House; and so he did, having the same well ordered and governed by his head Officers therein, and all things in plentiful manner, both for his own service and entertainment of Strangers, according to their several Qualities and Degrees. He often feasted the Clergy, Nobility, and Gentry of his Dioceses and Neighbourhood. And at Christmas, especially, his Gates were always open, and his Hall set twice or thrice over with Strangers: Upon some chief Festival days he was served with great solemnity, sometime upon the Knee, as well for the upholding of the State that belonged unto his Place, as for the better education and practice of his Gentlemen and Attendants in point of service.
>
> (103)

In the 1590s, hospitality to "strangers" was already a custom in decline even among the bishops. Therefore, the description above must have been the biographer's praise for Whitgift's generous hospitality. However, the biographer ironically reveals that Whitgift entertained the poor only at Christmas; during the rest of the year, he entertained "the clergy, nobility, and gentry of his dioceses and neighbourhood." Moreover, strangers were differentiated "according to their several qualities and degrees." Looking at this background, the final phase of the drama includes quite a serious satire on the patron.

After the last spendthrift reporter Bacchus provides comic relief, drinking and merrymaking with Will Summer, Summer appoints Autumn as his successor. Winter protests against this, and makes the most invective speech in the play. Winter criticizes Autumn's good hospitality, because "Eche one do plucke from him without controll" (1249). In other words, indiscriminate charity is criticized:

> [...] if a fellow licensed to beg
> Should all his life time go from faire to faire,
> And buy gape-seede, hauing no businesse else.
> (1336–38)

In Elizabethan churches, charity towards the poor neighbors was frequently counseled in sermons, the *Book of Common Prayer*, and other religious writings. However, indiscriminate support for the poor was not entirely accepted, because it partly originated from the Catholic notion of charity (Heal *Prelates* 262).

Winter's satiric comment on charity is further developed by Christmas. He enters without singing, and claims that hospitality is "now grown out of fashion." Christmas sharply criticizes that it is hypocrisy to make a feast to the poor only for the twelve days of Christmas. This is directly applicable to Whitgift's hospitality at Christmas.

> [...] A mans belly was
> not made for a poudring beefe tub: to feede the poore twelue
> dayes, & let them starue all the yeare after, would but stretch
> out the guts wider then they should be, & so make famine
> a bigger den in their bellies then he had before.
> (1640–44)

Moreover, he comically pleads that hospitality has decayed not because the nobility is illiberal, but because it is economically impossible for them to entertain the innumerable poor at every Christmas:

> *Christmas.* *Liberalitas liberalitate perit*; loue me a little
> and loue me long: [...] I haue dambd vp all my chimnies for
> feare, (though I burne nothing but small cole) my house
> should be set on fire with the smoake. I will not deny,
> but once in a dozen yeare, when there is a great rot of
> sheepe, and I know not what to do with them, I keepe open

house for all the beggers, in some of my out-yardes; marry, they must bring bread with them, I am no Baker.
(1697–1716)

According to George Paul's biography, Whitgift often invited the clergy, nobility and gentry to his house. If the original audience consisted of the members of these social classes, the play must have been highly satirical. Shortly after the play was performed, the patron-client relationship between Whitgift and Nashe ended. It is often conjectured that Whitgift was offended by this satirical entertainment. However, the social satire in Nashe's *Summer's Last Will and Testament* was nothing new for the audience of the time; similar kinds of plays were produced around 1590. Robert Wilson's *The Three Lords and Three Ladies of London* (1588), *The Three Ladies of London* (1590), *The Coblers Prophesie* (1594) as well as *A Merry Knack to Know a Knave* (1591) by anonymous can be categorized into the same group as *Summer's Last Will and Testament*. These plays are characterized by mixed genres, allegorical characterizations and didactic elements of the morality plays. The morality element is evident in the title of *The Three Lordes and Three Ladies of London* of the 1590 edition which includes "The Pleasant and Stately Morall"(Wilson *Edition*: title page of *Three Lords*). The structure of the moralities is borrowed to satirize the moral corruption as well as to idealize the past (Dynes). In *Three Ladies*, one of the allegorical figures, Hospitality, says, "My friend, hospitality doth not consist in great fare and banqueting, / But in doing good unto the poor, and to yield them some refreshing"(291). However, he is killed by Usury, saying "Farewell, Lady Conscience: you shall have Hos- / pitality in London nor England no more" (317). In *The Coblers Prophesie*, the Cobler says, "The chimnies so manie, and almes not anies" (323). In *A Merry Knack to Know a Knave*, Knight talks about the decay of hospitality and the idealized past:

> Neighbour Walter, I cannot but admire to see
> How housekeeping is decayed within this thirty year;

> But where the fault is, God knows: I know not.
> My father in his lifetime gave hospitality
> To all strangers,
> And distressed travelers;
> His table was never empty of bread, beef, and beer;
> He was wont to keep a hundred tall men in his hall.
> He was a feaster of all comers in general,
> And yet was he never in want of money: I think
> God did bless him with increase for his bountiful mind.
>
> (544)

It is clear that the declining hospitality, which was a popular subject of the age, was also thematized in the drama. The two plays examined in this chapter, *Summer's Last Will and Testament* and *The Old Wives Tale*, are rightly categorized into the hospitality plays.

III

Ancient Folkloric Romances

Festive drama was popular among a broad audience attending commercial theaters in London. Herculean characters such as Robin Hood and St. George, reminiscent of combat games of the May festival (Wickham 134–36; Laroque *Shakespeare's* 51–57), played a new role in the theater from the 1590s onwards. As discussed in the previous chapter, in Peele's festive fantasy, *The Old Wives Tale*, a didactic ending shows that charitable conduct is financially rewarded and results in a happy marriage. On the popular stage, the festive plot is directly related to the hero's social success. For example, disguises conceal the characters' identities and temporarily dissolve the social boundaries. A Herculean hero proves his courage and loyalty through man-to-man combat, and eventually acquires an honorable status to marry a woman of high rank. The following three festive plays, *George a Greene, the Pinner of Wakefield, Mucedorus* and *The Seven Champions of Christendom* are typical wish-fulfillment fantasies, which were perennially played in the Elizabethan and the Stuart periods.

1. George a Greene, the Pinner of Wakefield

George a Greene, the Pinner of Wakefield was entered in the Stationers' Register in 1595. There is only one surviving text printed in 1599. The title page shows that "it was sundry times acted by the seruants of the right Honourable the Earle of Sussex." [19] Then the play was acted by the Lord Admiral's Men at the Rose. According to Henslowe's diary, *George a Greene* was performed at least five times between 1593 and 1594 (Foakes 20).

The authorship is uncertain. However, some scholars have ascribed *George a Greene* to Robert Greene because of the handwritten inscription on the title page: "Ed. Juby saith that this play was made by Ro. Gree[ne]." Alan H. Nelson assumes that "Ed[ward] Juby" is an actor whose career is dated between 1594 and 1618 (74). However, another statement is inscribed on the title page: the play was "written by a minister, who ac[ted] the piners p[art] in it himself. Teste W. Shakespea[re]." Critics have hotly debated whether these inscriptions are authentic. From a paleographer's viewpoint, Nelson has recently insisted that both of them were written by George Buc, who was Master of the Revels from 1610 to 1622. Moreover, Nelson denies the authorship of Robert Greene, though testified by Juby, and concludes that *George a Greene* was an old play because even Buc, who was "a theater aficionado," did not know its author (74–83). In fact, there is no conclusive evidence to prove Greene's authorship. As is often suggested, the versification is much more awkward than in Greene's other plays (Collins 160–61; Adams 691).

George a Greene is a legendary hero, as sung in the ballad, "The Jolly Pinder of Wakefield" (T. Percy *Folio* 12; Ritson 2: 166–69; Knight *Outlaw Tales* 471–72). The song was entered in the Stationers' Register from 1557 to 1559 (Knight *Outlaw Tales* 469), and was very popular among contemporaries. Anthony Munday quoted it in his *The Downfall of Robert Earl of Huntington* (195). Pinder is a town official whose duties included impounding stray animals to protect the local crops. The ballad focuses on George's sturdiness in his combat against Robin, who was trespassing on "the kings highway" with his band of men, Scarlet and John. Their fight continued all day long, and Robin finally praises George as "one of the best pindèrs, / that ever I [he] tried with sword." Then Robin asks George to "forsake thy [his] pinders craft, / And live in the green-wood with me [Robin]" (Ritson 2: 168). The anonymous play *George a Greene* is clearly based on this ballad (M. Nelson 98–113; Knight *Robin Hood* 63), featuring the combat between George and Robin as well as Robin's invitation to join his band of men.

During the fifteenth and sixteenth centuries, Robin Hood games, such as combat and plays, were customarily held in local parishes for the purpose of collecting charity. According to churchwarden accounts and other local records, a churchwarden often played the part of Robin Hood and collected money (Johnston "Summer" 37–55; Johnston "What" 97; Stokes "Robin Hood" 1–25; Stokes "Processional" 242–48; Greenfield "Carnivalesque" 23–26). Then it seems likely that the original author of *George a Greene* is "a minister," who "acted the piner's part." Besides, considering Juby's testimony to Greene's authorship, the play may have been revised by Robert Greene to be added to the Admiral's Men's repertoires in the 1590s. This conjecture is reinforced by another old amateur play, of which revised version was acted by a professional company (Jackson "Edward" 245; Thornberry 362–64).

Mucedorus is an old play, which was not entered in the Stationers' Register until 1618. The text was printed at least 17 times between 1598 and 1668. The play was obviously popular. The oldest edition in existence is the 1598 quarto, and its title page shows that "it hath bin sundrie times plaide in the honorable Cittie of London"(*Mucedorus* 1598). This text does not specifically name the playing company. On the other hand, the 1610 edition clearly shows that the play was "Amplified with new additions, as it was acted before the Kings Maiestie at White-hall on Shroue-sunday night. By his Highnes Seruantes usually playing at the Globe" (*Most Pleasant*). It is no doubt that the revised edition of 1610 belonged to the King's Men. However, as E. K. Chambers suggests, there is no evidence to attribute the edition of 1598 to the Chamberlain's play.

The text is exceptionally short and the casting is conveniently made for doubling, so that it may have been suitable for performances by a small company of touring players. The 1598 play may have been acted by some disbanded company or strolling players (*Elizabethan* 4: 36).

It is recorded that some strolling players performed *Mucedorus* in the mid-seventeenth century. In 'A Briefe Narrative of the Play Acted at Witny the Third of February 1652. With its Sad and Tragicall End', John Rowe describes the accidental collapse of the old inn where *Mucedorus* was being acted. This was published with his sermons, which were preached to "the Inhabitants of the Towne, & Parish of Witny," under the title of *Tragi-comædia: Being a Brief Relation of the Strange, and Wonderfull Hand of God Discovered at Witny, in the Comedy Acted There Feburary the Third, Where There Were Some Slaine, Many Hurt, with Severall Other Remarkable Passages*. Rowe's reference to *Mucedorus* is nothing but a warning against the blasphemous performance of the play. However, his detailed record makes us conjecture that the play was still popular among the local audiences of the 1650s:

> This play [*Mucedorus*] was an old play, and had been Acted by some of Santon-Harcourt men many years since. [...] The Actors of the Play were Countreymen; most of them, and for any thing I can heare, all of Stanton-Harcourt Parish. The punctual time of their first Learning the Play, cannot be certainly set downe: but this we have been told, they had been learning it ever since Michaelmas, and had been Acting privately every week. This we are informed upon more certain grounds, that they began to Act it in a more publike manner about Christmas, and Acted it three or four times in their own Parish, they Acted it likewise in severall neighbowring Parishes, as Moore, Stanlake, Southleigh, Cumner. The last place that they came at was Witny.
>
> (The Narrative: 2)

Mucedorus, repeatedly printed until 1668, must have been popular among the local audiences as well as Londoners. The play was probably acted by amateur actors in many places even after the theaters were closed (Reynolds 265–67). There is further evidence that *Mucedorus* was still performed by local players between 1777 and 1884, as well as other popular folk plays such as *St. George and the Fiery Dragon* and *Valentine and Orson* (Chambers *English* 190–91).

Unlike *Mucedorus*, there survives only one text of *George a Greene*, it is difficult to know whether the play was popular. However, if Admiral's *George a Greene* was a revised version of the old amateur play, the revised part may be a key to understanding the taste of contemporary London audiences. Some critics have broadly attributed it to the vogue for professional Robin Hood plays in the 1590s, categorizing *George a Green* as one of them. For example, *Robin Hood and Little John and Robin Hood's Penn'orths* were anonymously entered in the Stationers' Register in the 1590s, although neither text has survived. George Peele's *Edward I*, Anthony Munday's *The Downfall of Robert Earle of Huntington* & *The Death of Robert Earl of Huntington* (even though the latter was probably coauthored with Henry Chettle), and *Look About You* are generally regarded as a series of Robin Hood plays. However, as is often discussed, Robin is not a central character in *George a Greene*, but only plays second string to George. Similarly, in *Edward I*, the role of Robin is extremely marginalized. More noticeably, in Munday's plays, Robin is not a traditional forest outlaw, but a decent aristocrat who is loyal to his sovereign, Richard I. The gentrification of Robin was a common feature of the professional Robin Hood plays of the 1590s (M. Nelson 80–190; Holt 159–62; Knight *Robin Hood* 115–34; Davenport 45–62; Singman 111–12).

However, gentrified Robin was not the exclusive trend of the seventeenth century. The forest outlaw was still popular in the ballads, circulating throughout the century (C. Hill 77–78). A prose work based on the ballad tradition was also published in 1678 under the title of *The Notable Birth and Gallant Atchiebements of That Remarkable Outlaw Robin Hood*

(W. Thomas 2: 91–137). Why then was Robin gentrified particularly in the theaters of the 1590s?

David Wiles supposes that Robin was not gentrified but conservatized because of the nationalistic social background of the 1590s (*Early Plays* 54). Stephen Knight also observes that the late sixteenth century was the time of "new conservative and authoritarian control," and that the conservatism in the Robin Hood tradition is quite plausible ("Which Way" 127). Knight further comments that *George a Greene* is also "a naïve patriotic drama," in which George's loyalty to King Edward is emphatically dramatized rather than his Herculean strength (*Robin Hood* 119–21). In the ballad, George immediately accepts Robin's invitation to join the Robin's band of men and live in "the green-wood" with him:

> "O wilt thou forsake the pinder his craft,
> And go to the green-wood with me?
> Thou shalt have a livery twice in the year,
> The one green, the other brown."
>
> "If Michaelmas day was come and gone,
> And my master had paid me my fee,
> Then would I set as little by him,
> As my master doth by me."
> (Ritson 169)

George has no hesitation in leaving his current office and becoming a member of the outlaw band.

In the play, Robin also asks George to forsake his current status:

> *Robin Hood.* George, wilt thou forsake Wakefield,
> And go with me?
> Two liueries will I giue thee euerie yeere,
> And fortie crownes shall be thy fee.
> (5.1. 987–90)

However, George does answer Robin: "Robin Hood! Next to king Edward" (995). Clearly, George is solely loyal to King Edward. Not accepting Robin's request, George invites Robin to his poor house to join a feast. The difference between the ballad and the play is also noted by Peter Stallybrass, who regards *George a Greene* as a drama of "the staunch upholder of good orders" (135).

As Knight and Stallybrass point out, George's loyalty to the King is repeatedly emphasized. It is most clearly shown in his conflict with the Earl of Kendal, who is the traitor to the King. Kendal also asks George to join his band of men:

> *Georg.* I, my Lord, considering me one thing, you will leaue
> these armes and follow your good King.
> *Ken.* Why, George, I rise not against King Edward, but for
> the poore that is opprest by wrong; and, if King Edward
> will redresse the same, I will not offer him disparagement, but
> otherwise; and so let this suffise. Thou hear'st the reason
> why I rise in armes: nowe, wilt thou leaue Wakefield and
> wend with me, Ile make thee captaine of a hardie band, and,
> when I haue my will, dubbe thee a knight.
>
> (2. 3. 500–08)

Kendal who pretends to be a savior of the poor is clearly a mock Robin Hood. The parody is more obvious in Kendal's request for George to "leaue Wakefield and wend with me [him]," which is reminiscent of Robin's offer to George. Ironically, George invites Kendall to his house and gives him "wafer cakes" and "a peece of beefe," although George's hospitality is only pretended. The most important parallel between Kendal and Robin is George's disregard to both invitations because of his absolute loyalty to King Edward. It is clear that George's allegiance to King Edward is the central theme of the drama.

The conservative elements in the Robin Hood plays of the 1590s may have partly reflected the rising nationalism at that time. However, *George a Greene* was persistently popular throughout the seventeenth century. The first evidence is found in the fragmentary theater record of the 17th century. In 1616, Christopher Beeston built a new indoor theater, the Cockpit, in Drury Lane in West End, for gathering the wealthy audiences of the Blackfriars and the Inns of Court students. When it was opened, several plays were taken from amphitheaters. Some of Thomas Heywood's plays were taken from the Red Bull, and Christopher Marlowe's *The Jew of Malta* was also moved from the Rose. *George a Greene* may have been one of them, because it is listed in the 1639 restraint of plays as Beeston's property. It is probable that *George a Greene* was still performed at the Cockpit in the 1630s (Gurr "Money" 10–11; Gurr "Amphitheatres" 53, 57).

The second evidence is a prose work, *The Famous Hystory off George a Greene, Pinder off the Towne off Wakefield*. The earliest extant text is the 1706 edition, but the work is dated between the late sixteenth and early seventeenth century (M. Nelson 98). As Nelson discusses in detail, *The History* has much in common with Munday's plays, particularly in the characterization of Robin and Maid Marian (100–01). However, the overall plot is similar to that of *George a Greene*, in that George's loyalty to King Edward is centrally dramatized. Since *The History* was published in 1706, the conservatized legend of George a Greene may have been popular until the end of the seventeenth century. Moreover, the play also continued to be acted at the Cockpit. Thus the durable popularity of *George a Greene* was not necessarily related to the patriotic background of the 1590s, but may have had another factor to attract the seventeenth century audiences.

The playwright created the episode of the shoemaker of Bradford, adding it to the basic story of the ballad. In Act V Scene I, the shoemaker stands in the way of King Edward and King James, who are passing through Bradford under the disguise of yeomen. Not knowing their identities, the shoemaker tells them not to hang their staves when they walk through the town but to trail them:

> This is the towne of merrie Bradford,
> And here hath beene a custome kept of olde,
> That none may beare his staffe vpon his necke,
> But traile it all along throughout the towne,
> Vnlesse they meane to haue a bout with me.
>   (5. 1. 1018–22)

The shoemaker clearly shows his allegiance to King Edward in his speech: "King or Kaisar, none shall passe this way, / Except King Edward" (5.1.1025–26). The shoemaker bravely makes the two kings "content to traile our [their] staues." When George and Robin, also in disguise, try to provoke the two disguised kings into fight, a band of shoemakers courageously guard the kings, fighting against George and Robin. In the last scene, after King Edward reveals his identity, the shoemakers' loyalty is rewarded by their honorable elevation to the "gentle-craft":

> *Ienkin.* Mary, because you haue drunke with the King, and the king hath so graciously pledgd you, you shall be no more called Shoomakers; but you and yours, to the worlds ende, shall be called the trade of the gentle craft.
>   (5. 1. 1135–38)

As seen in John Stow's *A Survey of London* of 1598, London merchants had become active by the end of the sixteenth century (Stevenson 77–91; Beier and Finlay 15–17). It may be against this background that the playwright inserted the shoemakers' heroic story probably in response to the sensitivities of the contemporary audience.

Over the last few decades, national and political contexts of Elizabethan theater have been much discussed. The argument of Stephen Knight and David Wiles, finding a correlation between George's conservatism and the nationalism of the 1590s, is a good example. However, looking at the commercial aspects of London theaters, they must have been closely related to the economic activity of the livery companies, rather than to national politics. Recent research has demonstrated that the development of professional theaters were in part due to London livery companies (Orgel 64–68; Kathman 1–49). A large percentage of the boy actors usually consisted of London apprentices, and the children's playing companies were managed by freemen who were independent of their guilds. In a record appears William Hunnis, a freeman of the Grocers, who worked as the leader of the Children of the Chapel Royal between 1566 and 1584 (Kathman 30). In *The Knight of the Burning Pestle*, the Citizen's Wife says that his son played *Mucedorus* "before the wardens of our [their] company" (Beaumont Induction 84). This suggests that the play was acted before the officers of the Grocers. The Wife's speech may not be completely fictional, but more or less reflects the contemporary theatrical context. Moreover, the apprentice players were usually freed of their livery companies when they become adult players, although they were trained exclusively for the stage, not for their crafts.

The livery companies' contribution to the development of the theater was not only the management of the playing companies, but also their performances in civic pageants and parish entertainments. Such guild shows may have influenced contemporary trends in theater. According to the record of the Wells Show of 1607, a series of charitable entertainments were held between May Day and Midsummer's Day. The event consisted of several traditional May games and fairly sophisticated plays acted by five livery companies. *The Pinner of Wakefield* is listed as one of the guild shows (Stokes "Wells Shows" 145–56). As there is no surviving detailed record of the performance, it is uncertain whether the play was connected with Admiral's *George a Greene*. However, the show was most likely to be performed by the shoemakers' company, the Cordwainers. This assumption is supported by another record of the guild entertainment in Somerset: the Cordwainers Show of 1613 (Stokes "Wells Cordwainers Show" 332–46). According to the record, the Cordwainers held a procession, a Morris Dance, a presentation of arms and a drama of St. Crispin and St. Crispianus, who are the patron saints of their company. These fragmentary records indicate that the Cordwainers, which were undoubtedly one of the traditional and powerful livery companies (Hazlitt *Livery* 449–56), regularly hold this kind of festive entertainment. *The Pinner of Wakefield* presented in 1607 may have been one of their plays. *George a Greene* acted at the Rose, in which the shoemakers' heroic story is inserted, was probably a timely repertoire for the guild-oriented audiences of London.

The close connection between the Cordwainers and the legend of George a Greene is also recognizable in another document. Richard Brathwaite, a poet who was born in north England, wrote several works about topographical features of his home country. In *A Strappado for the Diuell. Epigrams and Satyres Alluding to the Time, with Diuers Measures of No Lesse Delight* published in 1615, he refers to the legend of George a Greene in "To All True-bred Northerne Sparks, of the Generous Society of the Cottoneers, Who Hold Their High Roade by the Pinder of Wakefield, the Shoo-maker of Brandford, and the White Coate of Kendall: Light Gaines, Heauie Purses, Good Tradings, with Cleare Conscience":

> The first whereof that I intend to show,
> Is merry Wakefield and her Pindar too;
> Which Fame hath blaz'd with all that did belong,
> Vnto that Towne in many gladsome song:
> The Pindars valour and how firme he stood,
> In th' Townes defence 'gainst th' Rebel Robin-hood,
> How stoutly he behav'd himselfe, and would,
> In spite of Robin bring his horse to th' hold,
> His many May games which were to be seene,
> Yeerely presented vpon Wakefield greene.
>
> (203)

Brathwaite's description clearly shows that the legend of George a Greene was still popular in the seventeenth century. However, the author deplores that "the Pindars gone, / And of those jolly laddes that were, not one / Left to suruiue" (204), and quickly moves on to the next subject, "the jolly shoo-maker of Brad-ford towne":

> Vnto thy taske my *Muse*, and now make knowne,
> The iolly shoo-maker of Brad-ford towne,
> His gentle-craft so rais'd in former time
> By princely Iourney-men his discipline,
> Where he was wont with passengers to quaffe,
> But suffer none to carry up their staffe
> Vpon their shoulders, whilst they past through town
> For if they did he soon would beat them downe.
> (So valiant was the Souter) and from hence,
> Twixt Robin-hood and him grew th' difference;
> Which cause it is by most stage-poets writ,
> For breuity, I thought good to omit,
>
> (204–205)

The shoemakers' elevation to the "gentle-craft," dramatized in *George a Greene*, is mentioned above. Moreover, Brathwaite notes that "most stage-poets" write regarding the shoemakers' bravery. This statement implies that the shoemaker of Bradford had already become an important part of the legend of George a Greene by the early seventeenth century.

A shoemaker's successful career was a very familiar subject in contemporary literary works. Thomas Dekker's *The Shoemaker's Holiday or The Gentle Craft* was first performed by the Admiral's Men at the Rose in the late summer or autumn of 1599. The play is mainly based on Part One of Thomas Deloney's prose work, *The Gentle Craft*, which was first published in 1597, although the earliest text has not survived. Dekker's play celebrates the Cordwainers in the specific festive context of Shrove Tuesday. It is Dekker's original creation that Simon Eyre, who elevates to the Lord Mayor, makes a great feast for the King as well as for the shoemakers. The King, who is participating in the banquet, gives the shoemakers a "patent / To hold two market days in Leaden Hall (XXI 160–61)." This Saturnalian situation is similar to the last scene of *George a Greene*, in which King Edward drinks ale with a band of shoemakers, and allows them to become the gentle craft (Wiles "That Day" 51). William

Rowley's *A Shoemaker, A Gentleman* is also relevant to the Cordwainers. As the title page of the 1638 edition shows, the play was acted at the Red Bull and other theatres. The work is dated 1617–1618, when Rowley was the company holder of the Red Bull (Rowley x).

It was not only the shoemakers who were represented as heroic craftsmen. Thomas Deloney's *Jack of Newbury* is a story of a great clothier, Jack, who is renowned for his charitable deeds and great hospitality to the poor. In his *Thomas of Reading*, six worthy clothiers provide King Henry I with soldiers to fight against the French king. Richard Johnson's *The Nine Worthies of London* can be categorized into the same group. These examples suggest that there was a vogue for craftsmen's heroic stories, and that the insertion of the shoemakers' episode in *George a Greene* was probably part of this trend (Camp 13–23; Stevenson 107–30).

It has often been suggested that the vogue for the artisan's plays, probably originated in archetypal wish-fulfillment in a mobile society, clearly paralleled with the circulation of the popular myth of Richard/ Dick Whittington, who rose from the position of an artisan to the Lord Mayor of London (Barron 197–248; Burke "Popular" 156–57; L. Manley *London* 209–38; Bonahue 33–41; Robertson 51–66; Skura 166–68). Richard Whittington was born at Pauntley in Gloucestershire in the mid-fourteenth century. When his father died, he started to work as a London apprentice. Due to his talent as a mercer, he made a considerable fortune and became the Lord Mayor of London three times. In John Stow's *A Survey of London* (1598), Richard Whittington is mentioned as one of the worthiest citizens of England:

> Richard Whittington, mercer, three times mayor, in the year 1421 began the library of the Grey Friars in London, to the charge of four hundred pounds: his executors with his goods founded and built Whittington College, with almshouses for thirteen poor men, and divinity lectures to be read there for ever. They repaired St. Bartholomew's Hospital in Smithfield; they bare some charges to the glazing and paving of the Guild-

> hall; they bare half the charges of building the library there, and they built the west gate of London, of old time called Newgate, &c.
>
> (133)

The story of Whittington was repeatedly circulated in the seventeenth century. *The History of Richard Whittington, of His Lowe Byrth [and] His Great Fortune* was entered in the Stationers' Register in 1605. Although the text was lost, the record shows that 'yt was plaied by the prynces servants.' Five months later, a ballad, *The vertuous Lyfe and Memorable Death of Sir Richard Whittington Mercer sometymes Lord Maiour of the Honorable Citie of London*, was entered (Robertson 52), although the text has not survived. Richard Johnson wrote a poem about Whittington, 'Dainty, Come Thou to Me' in *A Crowne-Garland of Govlden Roses*, which was published in 1612. *The Famous and Remarkable History of Sir Richard Whittington* was probably written by Thomas Heywood and printed more than three times during the seventeenth century (Bonahue 40). Moreover, there are fragmentary references to Whittington in *If You Know Not Me, You Know Nobody* as well as in the induction of *The Knight of the Burning Pestle*. In the Lord Mayor's Show, patriotic and philanthropic mayors who rose from the craftsmen's ranks are often represented (Camp 13).

A. L. Beier and Roger Finlay suggest that the vogue for the Whittington story was closely related to the rapid increase of young migrants in London (21). There is a document that supports this hypothesis. A Puritan artisan, Nehemiah Wallington (1598–1658), left his personal record while he was bound to the Turners in London. Although his description focuses on religious matters, there is also valuable information on the contemporary society of guilds. For example, the Turners had about 265 apprentices between 1610 and 1620, and only 8.3 percent of them were Londoners (Seaver 68). This means that a large number of young apprentices migrated from other regions to London (Smith 149–61). Beier and Finlay further suggest:

We lack evidence for the exact age-structure of the population, but given the high level of immigration by young people and the importance of service and apprenticeship, adolescents were disproportionately numerous. There are in fact signs of a special youth culture geared to migrants and apprentices. […] Apprentices met regularly for meals and church services, and had their own holiday, Shrove Tuesday. […] The alehouse, the brothel and the theatre provided convenient venues for gatherings.

(21)

Both *George a Green* and *The Shoemaker's Holiday* were first acted at the Rose, the amphitheater playhouse whose admission fee was much lower than that of a hall playhouse. City apprentices and journeymen were probably the important clientele. This is also evident in the attack on the new indoor theater, the Cockpit, by a gang of apprentices on Shrove Tuesday in 1617, probably because they could not afford its high admission fee (Gurr *Shakespearian* 123–29). It is assumed that the idealization of the commonalty, the shoemakers and the pinders, was no less important than the absolute loyalty to King Edward in *George a Greene*.

From this viewpoint, George's allegiance to King Edward could be interpreted in a different way. Robin offers to pay George "fortie crownes" as an annual salary, if George forsakes his current office and becomes a member of Robin's band. In the ballad, George's salary is not mentioned at all. If it is the playwright's creation, the amount of 40 crowns may take on further implications. In Wallington's record, the cost of hiring an apprentice was at least about 6 pounds per year. A journeyman, who had finished his apprenticeship, was paid about 8 pounds (Seaver 68). Thus the annual payment of 40 crowns must have been an incredibly good condition for the pinder. However, George rejects Robin's offer. Instead, he is finally allowed to marry Grime's daughter, Bettris, and qualified to receive her father's lands because of his loyal deed. Moreover, George is bequeathed "half that Kendal hath" as well as "what as Bradford holdes of me [Edward] in chiefe" by King Edward. These rewards are far greater than the annual salary of 40 crowns.

As Richard Tardif significantly points out, the term 'yeoman' in the play should be considered in the urban context, "not only generally with reference to a specific class, but also as a particular rank within the organization of the guilds." Tardif further observes that "'an outlaw band of yeomen' is as much the description of a journeyman fraternity as it is a criminal band" (135). In other words, Robin's invitation to George represents a kind of headhunting in the craftsmen's society, in which translation to a different company was usual. On the other hand, George's disapproval of the negotiation comes out of his pride as a 'yeoman.' This is highlighted in the last scene, where he refuses to be dubbed a knight:

> *George.* Then let me liue and die a yeoman still:
> So was my father, so must liue his sonne.
> For tis more credite to men of base degree,
> To do great deeds, than men of dignitie.
> (5. 1. 1196–1199)

This attitude is also in common with his speech to Kendal, who regards George as "a base pinner" (2. 1. 245). George says, "A poore man that is true, is better / then an Earle, if he be false" (2. 3. 473–74). In fact, George's worthiness is proved when he declines to receive the ransom of the king of Scotland and insists that the money should be spent for charitable and civil purposes:

> *George.* Then let king Iames make good
> Those townes which he hath burnt vpon the borders;
> Giue a small pension to the fatherlesse,
> Whose fathers he caus'd murthered in those warres;
> Put in pledge for these things to your grace,
> And so returne.
> (5. 1. 1208–13)

George's honorable conduct is rightly reminiscent of the legendary hero, Richard Whittington, who was "base-born" and left his name in the history as the worthiest citizen of England.

George a Greene has long been regarded as one of the Robin Hood plays, which came out of the patriotic social background of the 1590s. However, George's conservatism, as well as the shoemakers', is much more relevant to the wish-fulfillment of the commonalty than the nationalism (Wright 623–24). Since the reign of Edward IV, the liaison between wealthy merchants and the monarch was well-established; the government relied on London merchants' investment and in return gave them profitable jobs, patents and monopolies (Beier & Finlay 15–16). On the other hand, as mentioned in the first chapter, the wealthy merchants' charitable contribution was remarkable. The merchant class endowed more than the gentry. In the play, George's noble mind is contrasted with Kendal's narrowness. The yeoman hero is idealized as a figure of courage, loyalty and hospitality, while Kendal who is of noble stock is far from a worthy figure. The conflict between birth and breeding in the mobile social classes is also an important theme in *Mucedorus* and *The Seven Champions of the Christendom*, which I examine below.

2. *Mucedorus*

Mucedorus was one of the most popular plays in the Elizabethan and the Stuart periods. As mentioned above, there are 17 surviving editions, which were printed between 1598 and 1668. The epilogue of the first quarto of 1598 suggests that the play was performed at Queen Elizabeth's court. The 1610 text shows that the play was performed by the King's Men at Whitehall on the night of Shrove Sunday. Thus the play was probably acted at the Globe, the home theater of the King's Men, and favored by a wide range of people. *Mucedorus* also continued to be performed as a popular entertainment in local parishes until the 19th century (Chambers *English* 190–91).

The wide and long-term popularity of the play may be partly attributed to its source, the folkloric love story of Mucedorus and Amadine, the prince of Valencia and the princess of Aragon. The story is about Mucedorus' adventurous wandering and romance with Amadine, and ends happily with their marriage. The circulation of the ballad, 'The Wandring Prince and Princess or, Musidorus and Amadine,' proves the popularity of the story. The song was published in 1676, included in *The Roxburghe Ballads* (Jupin 163–67). Although the date of the original creation is uncertain, the ballad is undoubtedly a later piece and has no direct relation with the play. However, both works, probably originating in the same folk roots (Brooke xxiii–xxv; Reynolds 266), may prove that *Mucedorus*' basic story was very popular and widely circulated for centuries.

There are some other elements to attract the 17th-century audiences. First, Bremo, a wild man of the woods is a key character. A wild man is originally a ritual figure in the pre-Christian world, representing natural power. He is associated with green leaves and a club. Bremo appears with his club in *Mucedorus*. During the 13th and 14th centuries, there was a vogue for the wild man in masques and court pageants. The first record is in the 1348 Christmas festivities of Edward III. By the beginning of the 16th century, the wild man became a familiar figure not only in such entertainments but also in the Midsummer pageants. Even after the Midsummer Watch was discontinued, the wild man still appeared in the Lord Mayor's procession, which was a great civic pageant of the year. He was at once a frightening and comic figure, brandishing torches. His main role was to clear the way for the procession. On St. George's Day in 1610, the City of Chester presented entertainments in honor of Prince Henry. It is recorded that wild men who were dressed in ivy and had clubs entertained the audience. Bremo, the wild man, must have been a familiar character to the Elizabethan audiences (Withington 72–77; Goldsmith 481–91; Unwin 274–75; Bergeron 30–32; Jupin 63–65; Laroque *Shakespeare's* 57).

However, Bremo represents not only primitiveness but also unworldly naivety or simple-minded defenselessness in *Mucedorus*. The moment he saw Amadine, he is charmed by her beauty and temporarily loses his cannibal instincts. Taking her to his woods, Bremo courts Amadine:

> If thou wilt love me, thou shalt be my queen;
> I will crown thee with a chaplet made of ivory,
> And make the rose and lily wait on thee. [...]
> The satyrs and the wood-nymphs shall attend on thee
> And lull thee asleep with music's sound,
> And in the morning when thou dost awake,
> The lark shall sing good morrow to my queen,
> And, whilst he sings, I'll kiss my Amadine. [...]
> And I will teach thee how to kill the deer,
> To chase the hart and how to rouse the roe,
> If thou wilt live to love and honor me.
> (xv. 24–26, 44–48, 53–55)[20]

Hearing Bremo's lengthy wooing, Amadine gives her aside several times: "You may, for who but you?" Bremo's persuasion is comic because the wild man's primitiveness is contrasted with the refinement of the princess. On the other hand, Bremo's speech represents the innocence of the pastoral life, which is completely lost from the civilized world. The idealization of the past and the disillusionment of the present are more clearly thematized in Mucedorus' Golden Age speech following Bremo's wooing scene:

> In time of yore, when men like brutish beasts
> Did lead their lives in loathsome cells and woods
> And wholly gave themselves to witless will,
> A rude, unruly rout, then man to man
> Became a present prey; then might prevailed;
> The weakest went to walls.
> Right was unknown, for wrong was all in all. [...]

> Instead of caves they built them castles strong;
> Cities and towns were founded by them then.
> Glad were they, they found such case, and in
> The end they grew to perfect amity.
> Weighing their former wickedness,
> They termed the time wherein they livèd then
> A golden age, a goodly golden age.
> (xv. 71–88)

Bremo is killed by Mucedorus, who is clever enough to disarm the wild man by pretending to learn how to use the weapon. Mucedorus' civilized intelligence triumphs over Bremo's primitiveness. Recollection of the Golden Age is a recurrent motif in Elizabethan literature. In *Mucedorus*, Bremo, a ritual character of the pre-Christian world, is not only a fictional element but also a vehicle to remind the audience of the social reality.

The Clown, Mouse, is another important character, who does not appear in the ballad but the playwright's creation. The importance of Mouse is noted in the supplementary description on the title page: "with the merry conceits of Mouse." Moreover, the part of Mouse was expanded in the 1610 edition, which probably reflects the taste of the contemporary audience (Jupin 38–39).

Mouse serves to keep detaching the audiences' attention from the dramatic illusion. Mouse's comments are particularly trenchant in his reference to mobile social classes. All of the characters except for Bremo are intensely concerned with title and occupation. The first instance is illustrated in the dialogue between Mouse and Segasto:

> *Mouse.* [...] I tell you, sir, I am the Goodman Rat's son of the next parish over the hill.
> *Seg.* Goodman Rat's son? Why, what's thy name?
> *Mouse.* Why, I am very near kin unto him.
> *Seg.* I think so, but what's thy name?
> *Mouse.* My name? I have a very pretty name. I'll

> tell you what my name is; my name is Mouse.
> *Seg.* What, plain Mouse?
> *Mouse.* Ay, plain Mouse without either welt or
> guard.[...]
>
> (iv. 65–74)

A name is an evidence to show whether one is titled. Segasto who belongs to the landed nobility thinks that "A merry man a merry master makes," and says to Mouse: "wilt thou dwell with me?" In this negotiation, Mouse would be given a new occupation and status. The following dialogue between Mouse and Segasto is further satiric:

> *Mouse.* Nay, soft, sir, two words to a bargain. Pray
> you, what occupation are you?
> *Seg.* No occupation; I live upon my lands.
> *Mouse.* Your lands? Away, you are no master for
> me. Why, do you think that I am so mad to go seek
> my living in the lands amongst the stones, briers, and
> bushes, and tear my holiday apparel? Not I, by your
> leave.
> *Seg.* Why, I do not mean thou shalt.
> *Mouse.* How then?
> *Seg.* Why, thou shalt be my man, and wait upon me
> at the court.
> *Mouse.* What's that?
> *Seg.* Where the King lies.
> *Mouse.* What's that same king, a man or a woman?
> *Seg.* A man as thou art.
> *Mouse.* As I am? Hark you, sir; pray you, what kin is
> he to Goodman King of our parish, the churchwarden?
> *Seg.* No kin to him; he is the King of the whole land.
> *Mouse.* King of the land! I never see him.
>
> (iv. 86–105)

Mouse repeatedly misconstrues Segasto's words, mocking his pride as a noble man. However, having been hired by Segasto, Mouse proudly refers to his title, "master," in introducing himself to Mucedorus. This time, Mucedorus mocks Mouse's pride by misunderstanding his words:

> *Mouse.* My name is called Master Mouse.
> *Mu.* Oh, Master Mouse, I pray you, what office
>   might you bear in the court?
> *Mouse.* Marry, sir, I am a rusher of the stable.
> *Mu.* Oh, usher of the table!
> (xiv. 58–62)

The matter of rank and occupation is also thematized in the main plot. Mucedorus and Segasto are rivals in love. Mucedorus, in disguise of a shepherd, kills a bear and helps Amadine. On the other hand, Segasto, who is of noble stock, runs away from the bear and deserts her. As the shepherd's courage is worthier than the nobleman's cowardice, Amadine wishes to marry Mucedorus. In the last scene, however, Mucedorus' disguised identity is problematized by Amadine's father, King of Aragon:

> *Mu.* I do deserve the daughter of a king.
> *King.* Oh, impudent! A shepherd and so insolent?
> *Mu.* No shepherd I, but a worthy prince.
> *King.* In fair conceit, not princely born.
> *Mu.* Yes, princely born: my father is a king,
>   My mother a queen, and of Valencia both.
> *King.* What, Mucedorus? Welcome to our court!
> (xviii. 50–56)

As Mucedorus turns out to be a man of noble stock, he is allowed to marry Amadine and become a prince of Valencia. This is decisively different from the happy-ending of a wish-fulfillment fantasy such as in *George a Greene*. In *Mucedorus*, the happy ending is not brought by the hero's social elevation but by the revelation of his real identity.

As *Mucedorus* was performed by the King's Men at the Globe, the audiences' demand may have been somewhat different from that of the Rose audiences. The diversified elements in *Mucedorus*: royal fantasy, folk ritual and social satire probably attracted a wide range of audiences.

It is generally agreed that the successful revival of *Mucedorus* caused a vogue for romance, and gave Shakespeare some ideas for his late plays (Frost 19–38; L. Manley *Literature* 433–44). In fact, there are similarities between *Mucedorus* and Shakespeare's late plays: a dichotomy between the civilized world and the innocence of nature, identity matter of disguised prince or princess, a happy ending in reunion and marriage. Compared with Shakespeare's Romances, *Mucedorus* is undeniably less sophisticated. However, the play was historically long-run particularly after the text was revised as King's Men's property. Shakespeare's late plays were produced in the same context around 1610. Before reexamining Shakespeare's late plays, I look at another festive romance, *The Seven Champions of Christendom*, which was performed at the Cockpit probably as an immediate reaction to the great success of Shakespeare's late plays.

3. *The Seven Champions of Christendom*

The title page of *The Seven Champions of Christendom* shows that the play was "acted at the Cocke-pit, and at the Red-Bull in St. Johns Streete, with a generall liking, and never printed till this yeare 1638."[21] Then the play was first acted at the Red Bull and continued to be played at the Cockpit, just as *George a Greene* was taken from the Rose by Christopher Beeston, as I mentioned above (Gurr "Amphitheatres" 57).

The date of the original creation is uncertain. Since the main source of the play is Richard Johnson's Part One of *The Most Famous History of the Seauen Champions of Christendom*, the play must have been written after the first publication of 1596. John Freehafer analyzes numerous topical allusions made in the play as well as the echoes from the contemporary works, and assumes that the work is dated between 1613 and 1614 (87–94). Freehafer's argument is reinforced by the Clown's reference to the Lancashire witches, which can be dated to 1612. In the play, the Clown, Suckabus, is the son of Tarpax, the Devil and Calib, the Witch. Suckabus is concerned with his birth, and asks his parents whether they are of noble stock:

> *Clow.* But doe you heare Father, if you be a Prince, I must
> be a Lord, or an Earle, or a devilish Duke, or somewhat.
> *Tar.* Thou art by birth Duke of Styx, Sulpher, & Helvetia.
> *Clow.* O brave, o brave, Duke of Styx, Sulpher, & Helvetia?
> Pray father, what Title hath my Mother?
> *Tar.* Queene of Limbony, and Dutchesse of Witchcordia.
> *Clow.* I thought so, I told my Mother shee lookt like a
> Witch a great while agoe: a poxe on't, I knew it: but doe
> you heare mother, were not you one of the Cats that drunke
> up the Millers Ale in Lancashire Wind-mills?
>
> (B3)

The last two lines obviously refer to the witches who were brought to trial in Lancashire. Some scholars regard this as an allusion to *The Late Lancashire Witches*, which was written by Thomas Heywood and Richard Brome and played at the Globe just after the second witch trial of 1634 (Gurr *Shakespearian* 146, 442). However, the Lancashire witch trial first took place in August 1612, and it was probably much more sensational than the 1634 case, because the accused witches were sentenced to death in the first trial. Its historical record was published in 1613 by Thomas Potts who was the judges' clerk at the trial of 1612. The witch story of 1612 likely provided good material for contemporary playwrights and pamphleteers in making topical allusions in their works. The Clown's reference to the Lancashire witches also may have been written shortly after the first trial of 1612 (Purkiss 233–34).

Ben Jonson refers to the witches in his *Bartholomew Fair*, which was performed on October 31, 1614: "The Wind-mill blowne downe by the witches fart!" (2.4.18)[22] This is the title of the ballad that Nightingale sells. This line is immediately followed by another reference to the ballad: "Or Saint George, that O! did breake the Dragons heart!" (2.4.19). Jonson harshly criticizes the current fashion of romance plays: "like those that beget *Tales, Tempests*, and such / like drolleries, to mix his head with other men's heels" (Induction 131–32) in *Bartholomew Fair*. It seems quite probable that *The Seven Champions* was alluded to in these two lines through the association between "the witch" and "St. George." If so, *The Seven Champions* must have been written before October 1614 and sometime after August 1612 (Freehafer 102).

As for the authorship, the title page shows that the play was "written by J. K." The signature at the end of the epistle dedicatory identifies the author with "John Kirke," who was an actor-manager of Prince Charles' Men at the Red Bull (Lawrence 586–93; Wright 618; Gurr *Shakespearian* 441–42). However, if the play was written around 1613, Kirke's authorship is questionable. Kirke was a strolling player in 1629 (Gurr *Shakespearian* 448) and could not have written a play around 1613. Freehafer assumes that Kirke was only involved in the process of the publication, and that the real author was Wentworth Smith, who wrote *The Hector of Germany* and other pseudo-historical works for Philip Henslowe. Freehafer's supposition is drawn from the following interrelated evidence. First, *The Hector of Germany*, in which "W. Smith" is inscribed, was dedicated to Sir John Swinnerton who became a Lord Mayor from the Merchant Taylor's Company. Secondly, the Company had the great honor of accepting Prince Henry as a member in 1607. In Richard Johnson's *A Crowne-Garland of Govlden Roses* (1612), Prince Henry is compared to St. George and his membership of the Merchant Taylors is celebrated:

> Saint Georges feast, the first of all,
>   maintained is by Kings:
> Where much renowne and royalty,

> thereof now dayly rings.
> Princes come from forraine lands,
>   to be Saint Georges Knights:
> The goulden garter thus is morne,
>   by sundry worthy mights.
>
> Saint George our English champion,
>   in most delightfull lost:
> Is celebrated yeare by yeare,
>   in Englands royall court.
> The King with all his noble traine,
>   in gould and rich aray,
> Still glorifies the festiuall,
>   Of great Saint Georges Day.
>   (A7)

Thirdly, Johnson's other work based on the legend of St. George, *The Most Famous History of the Seauen Champions of Christendom* is the source of *The Seven Champions*. Freehafer concludes that the manifold connection between Wentworth Smith and Richard Johnson may have led to the production of *The Seven Champions* (95–98).

However, Paul Merchant argues that the dedication to Swinnerton was not only made by Smith but also by other writers such as Anthony Munday, Thomas Dekker, Henry Peacham and John Taylor, who were all acquainted with Thomas Heywood. Then Smith's dedication to Swinnerton suggests a connection between Smith and Heywood. In fact, as Freehafer points out (94–95), there is both external and internal evidence to suggest Heywood's involvement in the production of *The Seven Champions*. On the grounds that the play has numerous echoes from the works of the 1590s and topical allusions of the period around 1613, Merchant concludes that *The Seven Champions* was originally written by Thomas Heywood in the 1590s, and was revised around 1613, mainly with the expansion of the role of the Clown (226–30).

Heywood's involvement in *The Seven Champions* is plausible, because the play was first performed at the Red Bull, where the Queen's Men acted between 1606 and 1616, managed by Beeston. Heywood's plays were the important repertoires. For example, *The Golden Age*, characterized by the ancient legendary material and the Clowne's topical allusions, has similarities with *The Seven Champions*. At the end of 1616, the Queen's Men moved to the Cockpit with Beeston, and acted there until 1619 (Gurr *Shakespearian* 124–27). It is also evident that Heywood retained links with Beeston at least until the early 1630s. Heywood's *The Silver Age*, which was originally a Red Bull play, was performed at the Cockpit in the late 1620s (Gurr "Amphitheatres" 60). The possibility of Heywood's authorship, at least of his collaborative involvement, is very strong.

Merchant's other supposition that the play was revised around 1613, with the addition of the Clown's topical allusions, is also plausible. The 1610 edition of *Mucedorus* is a similar precedent, in which Mouse's satirical role was expanded. Moreover, *The Seven Champions* has many similarities with *Mucedorus*. First, both plays are based on the ancient ballad. The source of *The Seven Champions* is the famous legend of St. George, from which Johnson's prose is also derived. However, the play's originality lies in the hero who shows particular interest in his birth. In the play, George asks his stepmother, Calib, whether his parents are of noble stock:

> *George.* Were they asham'd of their owne worke?
> How were they titled, Base or Noble pray?
> *Calib.* Base, and Noble too:
> Both base by thee, but noble by descent;
> And thou got base, yet maist thou write true gent:
> No further satisfaction seeke to know,
> I call thee George, thy sur-name I must not shew.
> (B4: Act1)

The playwright lets Calib avoid an immediate answer to prolong the revelation of the truth. Toward the end of the first Act, a dramatic situation is provided: the ghost of George's father reveals that George is "heire to the Earle of Coventry." In Johnson's *The Seauen Champions*, Kalyb immediately answers that George's father is "Lord Albert high Steward of England" (8). In the ballad of 'The Birth of St. George,' Lord Albert is the name of the Earl of Coventry:

> In Coventry sometime did dwell
> A knight of worthy fame,
> High steward of this noble realme;
> Lord Albert was his name.
> (T. Percy *Reliques* 9–12)

The ballad relates how George's mother "dreamt a dragon fierce and fell / Conceiv'd within her womb" (21–22) and died when he was born. Then George is stolen away by "the weird lady of the woods" (195). She "train'd him up in feates of armes, / And every martial play" (199–200). The basic setting of the play and the prose is based on this story. However, the class-conscious hero is completely the playwright's creation. The class-conscious element is also noticeable in the Clown's speeches. He is concerned with his origin, and asks his father whether he is a man of title such as: "a Lord, or an Earle, or a devilish Duke," as quoted above. More importantly, he often comments on the contemporary class-oriented society and distracts the audience's attention from the dramatic world, just like Mouse of *Mucedorus*.

The Clown's topical allusion appears most frequently in the third Act, where he reunites with George who was in prison for seven years. The Clown says that he served six masters in all during George's absence:

> Oh sir, I have had such a company of Masters in law
> since I left you: First sir, I serv'd a Lord till he entertain'd a
> Cooke, and then I must stay no longer: Then I was Gentleman Usher to a young Lady, but she hating new fashions, I

> hated her service. Then sir, I serv'd young Heire newly
> come to his Living, and because he open'd his gates, and let
> Hospitality enter, I bid than let to him: then I serv'd a Usu-
> rer, and because he would often be drunke, and let his An-
> gels flye gratis, I gave him the bag too: Then I dwelt with a
> Procter, and he every day would bid conscience to dinner,
> so there was no staying with him: Then I serv'd a Scrivener,
> but he was so taken up with his Orator the Pillary, that I was
> faine to leave him too: and then I came here a sheep-biting,
> as you see sir.
>
> (G: Act 3)

This is a catalogue of his former masters' occupations. The first three belong to the nobility or the landed gentry. Above all, the Clown's comment on the third master, "young Heire newly come to his Living" directly refers to the hospitality issue, which was highly topical during the Elizabethan and the Stuart periods. As discussed before, allusions to hospitality were closely associated with the nostalgia for the good old days. In this speech, the Clown's last trade is described as "sheep-biting," which is often represented as a pastoral innocence free from the vanity of civilized society. Just before this scene, the Clown enters "like a poore shepheard," and gives a soliloquy, which seems to be a parody of Mucedorus' Golden Age speech:

> [...] Oh my glorious Mother, what a time of
> eating had I in thy dayes, nay, my magnamious Master,
> whom I lost in the devils arse of Peake: what a plentifull
> progresse had I with thee, when we did nothing but kill Gy-
> ants and wild beasts, then the golden gobbets of Beefe and
> Bacon, [...]
>
> (F3)

More interestingly, the Clown's nostalgia for the plenty provisions of yore is presented immediately after the interruption by the Chorus, which economizes the action of seven years:

> Our Brittaine Knight we leave in his hard journey,
> But more hard attempt, yet all the other have not idle beene,
> For since their parting at the brazen Piller,
> Each hath shar'd strange and perillous adventures,
> Which here in severall acts to personate, would in the
> Meanest fill a larger Scene than on this Stage
> An Action would containe;
> But to the shortnesse of the time wee'le sort,
> Each Champion in't shall beare a little part
> Of their more larger History:
> Then let your fancies deeme upon a stage
> One man a thousand, and one houre an age.
>
> (F3)

This is rightly reminiscent of the Chorus in *The Winter's Tale*. Merchant points out that the Chorus' apology for the inadequacy of the stage is not new, but in common with Heywood's *The Fair Maid of the West* (229). Shakespeare's *Henry V* may be one of the precedents. However, the parody of *The Winter's Tale* is most evident in the comic dialogue between the Clown and the Shepherd, which immediately follows the Chorus in *The Seven Champions*, and vice versa in *The Winter's Tale* (Freehafer 92). Moreover, *The Seven Champions* is full of allusive comments on Shakespeare's *The Tempest* (Freehafer 98–101). We can assume that the third Act of *The Seven Champions* was written shortly after the great success of Shakespeare's last plays.

While King's Men performed the romance repertoires such as *Mucedorus* and Shakespeare's last plays at the Globe and probably *The Tempest* at the Blackfriars (Gurr "Tempest" 91–102), the Queen's Men competed with them by acting pseudo history plays like *The Ages* and *The Seven Champions* at the Red Bull. *The Golden Age* includes a spectacle of an eagle descending with Jupiter, which also appears in *Cymbeline*. The frequent use of dumb shows in *the Ages* is similar to that of *Pericles*. At the Hope, Jonson's *Bartholomew Fair* was played in rivalry with the romance plays. However, Jonson himself wrote in his 'Ode to Himselfe,' written after the failure of *The New Inne* (1629): "some mouldy tale, Like *Pericles*" (H. Percy and Evelyn Simpson 492 21–22) was outstandingly popular even twenty years after its first performance.

In this chapter, I have examined three plays, *George a Greene*, *Mucedorus* and *The Seven Champions of Christendom*, all of which are based on the ancient ballads and are reminiscent of the folk festive tradition, particularly the May festival. However, in each play, topical allusions, fused into the archaic stories, serve to juxtapose the past and the present. In *George a Greene*, the artisans' elevation is incorporated into the legend of Pinder of Wakefield. In *Mucedorus* and *The Seven Champions*, the Clown's satiric allusions to the mobile social classes are mixed into the folkloric romance and the heroic legend of St. George. In the next chapter, I focus on Shakespeare's *Pericles* and *The Winter's Tale*, in which unrealistic plot and setting, which are related to the ancient festive tradition, juxtapose the past and the present more skillfully.

IV

Shakespeare's Romances

1. *Pericles*

Perilces was entered in the Stationer's Register on 20 May 1608. The first quarto was published in 1609, suggesting that the play "hath been diuers and sundry times acted by his Maiesties Seruants, at the Globe on the Banck-side"(Shakespeare *Late*). George Wilkins' prose, *The Painfull Aduentures of Pericles, Prince of Tyre*, published in 1608, is referred to as "The true History of the Play of *Pericles*, as it was lately presented by the worthy and ancient Poet Iohn Gower." A record remains that Zorzi Giustinian, who was the Venetian ambassador between 5 January 1606 and 23 November 1608, saw the performance at the Globe. However, the London theaters were closed because of the plague from April to December in 1607 and again in the summer and autumn of 1608. Thus, the performance at the Globe can be dated in the first six months of 1608 (Delvecchio [1]; Gossett 1–2).

The title page of the 1609 quarto ascribes *Perilces* to Shakespeare. However, the play was not included in the First Folio of 1623. As it has long been discussed, there are stylistic differences between the first two acts and the last three. Recent research has focused on the fluidity of the play text; Mowat notes that texts were produced "through scripts, revisions, performances, clumsy notes or hazy flawed printed forms" (220). Gary Taylor and MacD. P. Jackson edited *A Reconstructed Text of Perilces*, based on the premise that the text was collaboratively written by Shakespeare and Wilkins, with the memory of several actors. However, Jackson suggests that other possible approaches are left for further research (*Defining* 190–217).

In spite of uncertainty about the authorship, *Perilces* was one of the most popular plays. There were as many as six quartos between 1609 and 1635. George Wilkins suggests in his argument of *Painfull Aduentures* that the play was highly successful: "Onely intreating the Reader to receiue this Historie in the same maner as it was vnder the habite of ancient *Gower* the famous English Poet, by the Kings Maiesties Palyers excellently presented" (7). An anonymous pamphlet of 1609, *Pimlico*, also refers to the popularity of *Perilces*:

> Amazed I stood to see a crowd
> Of civil throats stretched out so loud [...]
> So that I truly thought all these
> Came to see *Shore* or *Perilces*.
>   (Warren 1)

Ben Jonson indignantly comments on the great success of "some mouldy tale, Like *Perilces*" in his 'Ode to Himselfe.'

As Jonson describes, *Perilces* may have been characteristically old-fashioned. It is based on the ancient tale of Apolonius of Tyre, which was widely circulated during the Medieval and the Renaissance periods (Archibald 81–106). The basic story is mainly taken from Book VIII of John Gower's *Confessio Amantis* and Laurence Twine's *The Patterne of Painfull Adventures* (Bullough 6: 375–548). Above all, the debt to the *Confessio* is found in Gower's Chorus in the play. In *Confessio*, Gower gives a moral lesson against incestuous love between Antiochus and his daughter. In the play, Gower also moralizes the whole action in the Epilogue:

> In Antiochus and his daughter you have heard
> Of monstrous lust the due and just reward.
> In Pericles, his queen and daughter, seen,
> Although assail'd with fortune fierce and keen,
> Virtue [preserv'd] from fell destruction's blast,
> Led on by heaven, and crown'd with joy at last.
> (5. 3. 85–90)

Gower's Chorus, didactically recapitulating the action, is somewhat reminiscent of the medieval religious drama (Felperin 145; Mowat 220). However, his narration is not completely moralistic. As Hoenigman points out, the interplay between Gower and the playwright is particularly noticeable after the third act onward (461–79). Moreover, the play contains many topical elements of the playwright's creation, in addition to Gower's archaic moral story. The fishermen's lively conversation on the coast of Pentapolis and the description of the brothel in Meteline directly reflect the social reality of contemporary England. As I discussed in the previous chapter, the mobility of the social classes is often alluded to in the old-fashioned festive plays such as *George a Greene* and *The Seven Champions*. It may also be probable that Gower's Chorus, seemingly moralizing the ongoing action, serves to juxtapose off-stage reality with the ancient fictional world.

For example, the device is recognizable in his first Chorus.

> *Gow.* To sing a song that old was sung,
>   From ashes ancient Gower is come,
>   Assuming man's infirmities,
>   To glad your ear and please your eyes.
>   It hath been sung at festivals,
>   On ember-eves and holy [-ales];
>   And lords and ladies in their lives

> Have read it for restoratives.
> The purchase it to make men glorious,
> *Et bonum quo antiquius, eo melius.*
> If you, born in those latter times,
> When wit's more ripe, accept my rhymes,
> And that to hear an old man sing
> May to your wishes pleasure bring,
> I life would wish, and that I might
> Waste it for you like taper-light.
> (Act1. Chorus 1–16)

Gower says that he has risen from the dead to recite the old song. His versification is deliberately archaic, reminding the audiences that the following action is told by the dead medieval poet. The archaism is further stressed by the proverbial Latin tag: "the older a good thing is, the better" (Delvecchio [85] n.10; Gossett 172 n.10). Gower's words are apparently antiquated; at the same time they have multi-layered connotations. First, Gower says that he comes from "ashes," which directly mean his own dust. In addition, ashes are associated with man's mortal constitution, as well as a sign of penitence, as in the ceremony of Ash Wednesday. In the last scene, Pericles reunites with his daughter and wife, who were thought to be dead, having grievously fasted for three months. His repentance for their death and the celebration of their rebirth are central themes of the play. *Perilces* was acted at the Globe sometime in the first six months of 1608, and the performance may have occurred during Lent, the forty-day period of abstinence, fasting and repentance from Ash Wednesday to Easter, when the Resurrection is celebrated. In addition, the play was being performed at the reopened theater shortly after a long period of disastrous plague. According to one record, London was also suffering from a period of unusually cold weather: "the Thames began to put on his "freeze-coat," which he yet wears, about the week before Christmas; and hath kept it on till now this latter end of January [1608]" (*Great Frost* 169). Gower's statement that the play would be "restorative" for people is rightly suitable for the original audiences.

More importantly, Gower refers to the two specific festive occasions in the Church calendar, "ember-eves" and "holy-ales," when the song was often recited. Howard Felperin suggests that the references to the Church calendar as well as the Latin proverb "serve to surround the tale with an air of revered antiquity" (146). Neither Suzanne Gossett nor Doreen Delvecchio, who have recently edited *Perilces*, explains why these particular events are mentioned here, although they make a detailed note on each term. However, Gower's references to these festive occasions are not accidental. According to the *OED*, "ember" means a revolution of time, deriving from the Anglo-Saxon *ymb-ren*. The word is defined as "the English name of the four periods of fasting and prayer appointed by the Church to be observed respectively in the four seasons of the year. Since the Council of Placentia A. D. 1095, the Ember days have been the Wednesday and the following Friday and Saturday next following (1) the first Sunday in Lent, (2) Whitsunday, (3) Holy Cross Day, 14 Sep, (4) St. Lucia's Day, 13 Dec"('Ember', n^2). The origin is too ancient to define precisely, but the relation between ember-eves and fasting is clear. Moreover, fasting was closely connected to alms-giving in the Elizabethan ecclesiastical context. Particularly in time of dearth and famine, sober and abstinent diet was strongly advised to relieve the poor. The campaign culminated in the order issued by the Privy Council in Christmas 1596. The parish clergy preached in favor of fasting, hospitality and individual alms-giving to the needy on Wednesday and Friday evenings (Hindle "Dearth" 44–86; McIntosh 462). Although fasting for poor relief seems to have been restricted to fish days, Ember days and Lent by 1630, the association between ember-eves and hospitality may have been unmistakable for contemporary audiences.

"Holy-ales" are also traditionally charitable occasions. It is best known as the Whitsun church-ale, the money-raising festivity for general poor relief. In the medieval days, there were several kinds of charity ales, such as a help-ale or a bid-ale. People gathered to drink ale and raise funds for their poor neighbors. Although these communal festivities became less common in the early modern period, they were not completely abolished. In Cornwall, a church-ale festivity was held in 1602. In 1633, William Piers, bishop of Bath and Wells, wrote to Archbishop Laud to defend the custom against Puritans' objection, insisting that church-ale festivities are very beneficial both for the church and the poor (Clark *Alehouse* 151–57; Bennet 19–41).

It is worth noting that hospitality is symbolically presented before and after Gower's second Chorus. In Act 1, Scene 4, Cleon describes the serious famine at Tharsus in the conversation with his wife, as if to tell a sad tale to her. Cleon says that Tharsus was "A city on whom plenty held full hand, / For riches strew'd herself even in her streets" (1. 4. 22–23). However, the people forgot the gratitude for their peace and plenty, and "All poverty was scorn'd, and pride so great, / The name of help grew odious to repeat" (1. 4. 30–31). Cleon laments that his country is "now starv'd for want of exercise" (1. 4. 38). However, Cleon's sad 'tale' is suddenly interrupted by the arrival of Pericles, who mercifully gives his provisions to the neighboring nation:

> *Per.* Lord Govenor, for so we hear you are,
> Let not our ships and number of our men
> Be like a beacon fir'd t' amaze your eyes.
> We have heard your miseries as far as Tyre,
> And seen the desolation of your streets;
> Nor come we to add sorrow to your tears,
> But to relieve them of their heavy load;
> And these our ships, you happily may think
> Are like the Troyan horse was stuff'd within
> With bloody veins, expecting overthrow,
> Are stor'd with corn to make your needy bread,
> And give them life whom hunger starv'd half dead.
> (1. 4. 85–96)

The scene of Tharsus ends without giving any information about how the country was restored from misery. Instead, Gower appears and briefly reports that Pericles "is still at Tharsus, where each man / Thinks all is writ he [speken] can; / And, to remember what he does, / Build his statue to make him glorious" (2. 1. 11–14).

According to Twine's *Patterne*, Pericles does not give but sells wheat in a low price to the people of Tharsus, pretending to be a merchant. Revealing his identity as a prince, he returns all of the money to them so that they may reconstruct their city. In gratitude, people:

> erected in the market place a monument in the memoriall of him, his stature made of brasse standing in a charret, holding corne in his right hand, and spurning it with his left foot: and on the baser foot of the pillar whereon it stoode, was ingraven in great letters this superscription: Apollonius prince of Tirus gave a gift unto the citie of Tharsus whereby hee delivered it from a cruel death.
>
> (Bullough 6:433)

Wilkins' prose gives further explanation about Pericles' charitable contribution. Even the price of the wheat is specified: "each man paying for euery bushell eight peeces of brasse" (27). In the play, however, Pericles' benevolence is didactically narrated by Gower only as a virtue of a noble prince in the ancient fictional tale.

Hospitality is again dramatized immediately after the Chorus, but in quite a different manner from the previous scene. Pericles, thrown on the beach of Pentapolis, has to ask for hospitality from the fishermen on the coast:

> *Per.* A man, whom both the waters and the wind,
> In that vast tennis-court, hath made the ball
> For them to play upon, entreats you pity him.
> He asks of you that never us'd to beg.
> *1 Fish.* No, friend, cannot you beg? Here's them

> in our country of Greece gets more with begging than
> we can do with working.
>
> (2. 1. 59–65)

Taking Pericles for a real beggar, one of the fishermen ironically says that beggars can make a better living than honest labors in Greece. The original audiences must have recognized what the fisherman says as the real problem of the poor in England. After the enactment of the 1597 Act, poor relief became a statutory obligation of parishes, and a new tax system was introduced. However, the aid was given only to the 'deserving poor,' who were physically incapable of working and also well-behaved members of the local community. As a result, a number of idle beggars wandered from one place to another, seeking a meal and handouts. They were generally regarded as a threat to civil order and whipped before being expelled (McIntosh 457–68). It is totally ironic that Pericles, who is dressed like a beggar, surprisingly asks: "Why, are [your] beggars whipt then?" (2. 1. 90).

Another fisherman also implies that there are many idle beggars who take advantage of people's goodwill:

> *Per.* [*Aside*] How from the [finny] subject of the sea
> These fishers tell the infirmities of men,
> And from their wat'ry empire recollect
> All that may men approve or men detect!–
> Peace be at your labor, honest fishermen.
> *2 Fish.* Honest, good fellow, what's that? If it be
> a day fits you, search out of the calendar, and nobody
> look after it.
>
> (2. 1. 48–55)

"If it be a day fits you" has been a puzzling line, and many critics attribute it to the textual flaw (DelVecchio [111] n.50–51; Gossett 228 n.52–54). *OED* defines "to fit" as "to supply, furnish, or provide with what is fit, suitable, convenient, or necessary" ('fit', v¹., IV. 11. a). The fisherman's speech above is a direct reaction to the beggar words, "honest fishermen." Thus, "a day fits you" means a day when dishonest beggars, like Pericles, are fed without honest laboring. The day may refer to one of the Ember days in the church calendar. As the fishermen were talking about "drones/that rob the bee of her honey" just before Pericles appears, his response to Pericles/the beggar can be interpreted in the context of the poor relief.

However, the fishermen's mocking responses to Pericles do not come from their mercilessness. He actually receives generous hospitality from them: "Come, thou / shalt go home, and we'll have flesh for [holidays], fish / for fasting-days, and, moreo'er, puddings and flap- / jacks, and thou shalt be welcome" (2. 1. 80–83). What is suggested here is the fishermen's complaint of social injustices prevailing in the money-oriented society. It is also evident from another fisherman's satirical comment on the "rich-misers":

> *1 Fish.* Why, as men do a-land; the great ones eat
> up the little ones. I can compare our rich misers to
> nothing so fitly as to a whale: 'a plays and tumbles,
> driving the poor fry before him, and at last devour
> them all at a mouthful. Such whales have I heard on
> a' th' land, who never leave gaping till they swallow'd
> the whole parish, church, steeple, bells, and all.
> (2. 1. 28–34)

They also complain that "a poor man's right in the law" is hardly protected. The fishermen's scene follows immediately after Gower's archaic narration, and their topical allusions may stand out all the more. At the same time, however, their satire on the off-stage reality may be tactfully fused into Gower's moralized tale without giving any offense. The archaic setting situated by Gower serves to present a controversial issue less offensively in the play.

Corruption of the morality was a familiar subject in contemporary literature. Nicholas Breton's *A Merrie Dialogve betwixt The Taker and Mistaker* was first published in 1603 and again in 1635. According to the author, "the takers" are cunning men "who take themselues to be wise with a little wit, & rich with a little wealth" (A3), while "the mistakers" are honest men who are often deceived by the takers. The work consists of a comic dialogue between the two travelers who are discussing how people are easily mistaken. A sailor who was thrown on the beach by the tempest, like Pericles, asks for hospitality in front of "a goodly, faire, & gorgeously built house" (4). However, a "Mocke-begger" appears and says: "Sir, you are mistaken, this is a banqueting house, where the gazers are onely fed with conceipts, for there is not a chimney that smokes, nor a doore open, it is called Mock-begger, ha, ha, ha" (5). The dialogue is concluded by the list of the following ironic counsels:

> And last of all, take heed of a whore, a paire of dice, a parasite, a pandor, a cheater, a flatterer, and a promoter. Take a Courtier for a fine man, a Lawyer for a wise man, a Souldier for a valiant man, a Diuine for a learned man, a Merchant for a rich man, a clowne for a painefull man, and a begger for a poore man:
> (29)

Barnabee Rych's *The Honestie of This Age*, published in 1614, is also a satirical discourse on a dishonest society. Rych ironically comments:

> I have heard speaking of the *Golden Age* of the worlde, and some will say it is long sithens past, yet some others doe thinke, that the true golden age (indeed) was neuer till now, when gold and gifts doe compasse all things: but if I might giue my censure, I would call this, the *Honest age of the world*.
> (3)

Rych enumerates every kind of dishonesty:

But is not this an *honest Age*, when ougly vice doth beare the name of seemely virtue, when *Drunkennes* is called *Good fellowship*, *Murther* reputed for *Manhoode*, *Lechery*, is called *Honest love*, *Impudency Good audacitie*, *Pride* they say is *Decency*, and wretched *Misery*, they call *Good Husbandry*, *Hypocrisie*, they call *Sinceritie*, and *Flattery*, doth beare the name of *Eloquence*, *Truth*, and *Veritie*, and that which our predecessors would call flat *Knavery*, passeth now by the name of wit and policy.

(5–6)

Similarly in Thomas Middleton's *A Chaste Maid in Cheapside*, the clear-cut distinction between honesty and dishonesty is comically blurred, as repeatedly suggested by the joke that "a whore is proved to be an honest woman." It is also symbolic that the watermen in conspiracy of gentleman's dishonesty are rewarded by a French crown and called "honest fellows."

These backgrounds place the brothel scene in *Perilces* in the context of the contemporary moral debate. First, the dialogue among the Bawd, the Pander and Boult in Act 4, Scene 2, is worth analyzing:

> *Pand.* Search the market narrowly, Meteline is full
> of gallants. We lost too much money this mart by
> being too wenchless.
> *Bawd.* We were never so much out of creatures.
> We have but poor three, and they can do no more than
> they can do; and they with continual action are even
> as good as rotten.
> *Pand.* Therefore let's have fresh ones, what e'er we
> pay for them. If there be not a conscience to be us'd in
> every trade, we shall never prosper.
>
> (4. 2. 3–12)

They suggest that prostitution is a profitable "trade," if they only have "fresh" whores. However, the Bawd complains that they are now almost out of stock. Then Boult goes to the market, and pays a large sum for buying Marina, because he reckons that she is greatly profitable. Marina is not only a "virgin," but also "has a good face, speaks well, and has / excellent good clothes." The Pander says that prostitution is not an easy business: "O, our credit comes not in like the com- / modity, nor the commodity wages not with the danger" (4. 2. 30–31). However, the Bawd says: "Come, other sorts offend as well as we" (4. 2. 36).

According to Rych's *Honestie*, a brothel house was a facility no less required and profitable than an ale house or a tobacco house (28). After the last municipal brothel, the Southwark Stews, was closed in 1546, all forms of prostitution were officially banned. However, prostitution flourished as a private business. The brothel houses were distributed widely throughout London, not only in specific areas but also in the better-governed areas under the City's jurisdiction. Thus a cozy relationship between the authorities and the illicit business is indicated. It is also likely that a virgin was treated as a precious commodity for both keeper and client (McMullan 117–42; Griffiths 43–47). The brothel scene of *Perilces* may more or less reflect contemporary urban society.

However, unlike contemporary plays such as *A Chaste Maid*, a gentlewoman is markedly differentiated from a whore in *Perilces*. Marina advises the Bawd to be "an honest woman, or not a woman" (4. 2. 85). Moreover, Marina escapes from her plight by teaching her "virtues," such as singing, weaving, sewing and dancing, to the "honest women" of Meteline. The distinction between honesty and dishonesty is most clearly shown in Act 4, Scene 6, where Lysimachus, the governor of Meteline, comes to the brothel. The Bawd mentions that she is bound to Lysimachus. This implies that the governor is one of the most frequent customers of the brothel. Lysimachus' following speech exposes the corruption of the authority:

[…] O, you have heard
something of my power, and so stand [aloof] for more

serious wooing. But I protest to thee, pretty one, my authority shall not see thee, or else look friendly upon thee. Come bring me to some private place.

(4. 6. 86–90)

However, Marina warns against Lysimachus' dishonesty with a dignified manner: "If you were born to honor, show it now; / If put upon you, make the judgment good / That thought you worthy of it" (4. 6. 92–94).

In Twine's *Patterne*, the princess in the brothel is much more a feasible and pathetic character than Marina. She weeps and kneels down more than once, pleading for mercy on her virginity. It is a gentleman's compassion that finally relieves her from the brothel house. The heroine's chastity is the most important theme in the *Patterne*, as shown in the didactic ending: the virtuous princess becomes happy and the evil Bawd is burnt to death.

In contrast, the dialogue between Marina and Lysimachus is thoroughly comic, as Marina deliberately misconstrues what Lysimachus suggests:

> *Lys.* Now, pretty one, how long have you been at this trade?
> *Mar.* What trade, sir?
> *Lys.* Why, I cannot name['t] but I shall offend.
> *Mar.* I cannot be offended with my trade. Please you to name it.
> *Lys.* How long have you been of this profession?
> *Mar.* E'er since I can remember.
>
> (4. 6. 66–73)

More strikingly, having been preached by Marina, Lysimachus completely transforms into an honest gentleman, and generously bestows gold to the virtuous whore:

> *Mar.*   For me,

> That am a maid, though most ungentle fortune
> Have plac'd me in this sty, where since I came,
> Disease have been sold dearer than physic —
> That the gods
> Would set me free from this unhallowed place,
> Though they did change me to the meanest bird
> That flies i' th' purer air!
> Lys.   I did not think
> Thou couldst have spoke so well, ne'er dreamt thou couldst.
> Had I brought hither a corrupted mind,
> Thy speech had altered it. Hold, here's gold for thee.
> Preserver in that clear way thou goest,
> And the gods strengthen thee!
>
> (4. 6. 95–107)

The scene gives no explanation why Lysimachus is suddenly moved by Marina's speech. He only suggests that the whore "spoke so well" that he listened with wonder to her speech. Using hypothetical expression, Lysimachus implies that he has not come to the brothel with "a corrupted mind." However, his conversation with Boult and the Bawd clearly shows that he is a frequent customer of the brothel. As Delvecchio and Gossett comments ([170] n.96–107; 356 n.108–09), Lysimachus' false statement is probably the product of his embarrassment at being reproached by the virtuous maid. Furthermore, Lysimachus lies again and endows "more gold" to Marina as if to redeem his honor:

> Lys. For me, be you thoughten
> That I came with no ill intent, for to me
> The very doors and windows savor vilely.
> Fare thee well, thou art a piece of virtue, and
> I doubt not but thy training hath been noble.
> Hold, here's more gold for thee.
>
> (4. 6. 108–13)

Lysimachus' repentance for his dishonesty is caricatured in this scene.

The satire of the wealthy gentlemen's immorality is also evident in the clients who come to the brothel, to which Marina was sold, because all of them all wealthy gentlemen: a Spaniard "with his best ruff on," the French knight who is likely to "scatter his crowns" and Lysimachus who "will line your [Mariana's] apron / with gold." The Bawd tells Marina to enjoy "gentlemen of all fashions." It is true that prostitution was closely tied to the leisure habits of wealthy gentlemen and that becoming a private mistress of the wealthy men was a prominent mode of prostitution(McMullan 120–22).

However, prostitution was not a particular pleasure of the wealthy gentlemen. Paul Griffiths has recently researched the social profile of clientele of the brothel houses, based on the records of Bridewell. The research covers a sample of 219 clients, who are broadly divided into six groups: apprentices and servants (39.3%), craftsmen and tradesmen (12.3%), gentlemen and foreign merchants (11.4%), ambassadors' retinues (7.8%), the servants of bishops and aristocrats (5.0%) and young men of the Inns (3.2%). The data shows that the majority of clients were young males, who belonged to the lower classes. In *Northward Ho*, the bawd's best clients are tailors and apprentices. Supposing that Griffiths' analysis is true, the picture of *Northward Ho* might have been much closer to contemporary reality (55).

Griffiths also notices a close relationship between the flourishing prostitution business and the increasing number of young migrates in London, and assumes that the brothel houses had a significant relationship with youth culture. Griffiths further mentions that a story of prostitution in the contemporary prose and drama is often ideologically painted, making prostitution a particular pattern of social behavior (41). He suggests: "the world of prostitution had a clear place in the fabric of London society. Some keepers and pimps had a role in the capital's occupational structure. Further, commercial sex provided a social and sexual option for some sections of the 'integrated' society" (55–56).

Looking at this background, the moral conflict between the virtuous whore and the corrupted gentleman in *Perilces* may have been rather old-fashioned for the audiences at the Globe. Lysimachus' sudden repentance as well as Marina's preaching in the brothel house is totally unrealistic. Then Gower's Chorus serves to dissolve the absurdity. In Act 4, Gower appears twice — In the middle of the fourth act, Gower again reminds the audiences that the play is nothing but a tale told by a dead medieval poet. Then immediately after the Chorus, unrealistic transformation in the brothel house is told in the dialogue between the two gentlemen. They refer to Marina's marvelous preaching:

> 1 Gent. Did you ever hear the like?
> 2 Gent. No, nor never shall do in such a place as
> this, she being once gone.
> 1 Gent. But to have divinity preach'd there! did
> you ever dream of such a thing?
> 2 Gent. No, no. Come, I am for no more bawdy-
> houses. Shall's go hear the vestals sing?
> 1 Gent. I'll do any thing now that is virtuous,
> but I am out of the road of rutting for ever.
> (4. 5. 1–9)

The device is similar to the three gentlemen's narration, which is given prior to Hermione's wondrous transformation in *The Winter's Tale*. Thus Lysimachus' sudden regeneration is not illogical in the framework of Gower's moralizing tale. The play ends happily with a miraculous reunion of the virtuous family. Moreover, a happy marriage between Marina and Lysimachus is expected. However, the perfectly idealized ending itself covertly reinforces the fact that the play is nothing but a fiction. The nostalgia for the ancient moralized tale and the satire of the current dishonest society are the opposite side of the same coin.

2. *The Winter's Tale*

In Act 3, Scene 3, the stage direction suggests that Antigonus exits pursued by a bear. Following his exit, a comic conversation between the old Shepherd and the young Clown is inserted, reporting that Antigonus was torn to pieces by the bear. The scene has aroused much discussion among critics (Orgel *Winter's* 155–56 n.57.I). The first question is whether a real bear appeared on the stage. As bearbaiting was one of the most popular entertainments, the bear on stage may have been a tame one, which was brought from the nearby Bear-Pit in Southwark. Another possibility is that an actor dressed in bearskin chased Antigonus. The unexpected appearance of a real bear, even if it was not wild, may have shocked and frightened the audience. If the bear was counterfeit, the scene must have been too awkward to be accepted seriously. In any case, the bear trick in Act 3, Scene 3 serves to detach the audience's attention from the dramatic illusion.

There are a number of possible reasons that such a device is inserted in the middle of the play. Since the first half of the play is tragic and the other half is comic, the bear episode is a turning point from tragedy to comedy (Gurr "Bear" 420–25; Randall "Chase" 89–95). As Louise G. Clubb points out, bears frequently appeared in sixteenth-century pastoral tragicomedy (17–30). The bear device in *The Winter's Tale* may have been part of this trend. The transition from tragedy to comedy is also implied by the Shepherd, who says: "thou met'st with / things dying, I with things new-born" (3. 3. 113–14). Christopher Hardman notes that this is an echo of Evanthius' definitions of tragedy and comedy in *De Tragoedia et Comedia*, which was commonly cited in grammar school textbooks (10). The bear's appearance in Act 3, Scene 3 may have been a teasing device to show that the play was a 'fashionable' tragicomedy.

The bear scene has another important effect on the audience's psychological reception. After Antigonus' exit, the Clown comically reports that the bear made prey of Antigonus, as if he were telling a fictional tale. At the same time, a newborn baby found by the Shepherd enables the audience to anticipate that a new dramatic sequence has started. Thus, the audience's attention is gradually detached from the first half tragic sequence at Leontes' court, so that they can smoothly respond to the second-half comic development of the play. In other words, Act 3, Scene 3 makes a psychological transition of the audience's reception (Sasayama 91–105).

Bears were directly associated with festive enjoyment in early modern England. Wakes, fairs and bearbaitings were still popular activities in many localities. Recent research has categorized baiting into theatrical entertainment, and there are many references to baiting in *REED*. The records show that baiting most frequently and widely occurred in the county of Somerset between the 1530s and 1620s (Stokes "Bull" 65–80). They were mostly held in May and June in connection with Whitsun or Midsummer ales. The next most frequent presentments for baiting occurred in July, August and September, having linkage with ales, revels and the feasts of the local patron saints. In other words, baiting was held as a part of fund-raising entertainments in parish communities. There is much evidence to show that many baiters were accused of violating the Sabbath, because the events were traditionally held on Sundays. In the first decade of the seventeenth century, however, many parishes moved them from Sundays to another day of the week in order to avoid suppression.

Against this background, the bear episode seems to be a prelude to the festive rejoicings in the second half of the drama. Shortly after the bear's appearance, the setting moves to sheep-shearing in the countryside of Bohemia. The pastoral celebration signifies not only the seasonal transition from winter to spring, but also the agricultural lifecycle, death/rebirth, which is symbolically related to the central theme of the play. The baby whose name is Perdita signifying "lost" is brought up by the Shepherd and reached maturity. In the sheep-shearing, playing the queen of the feast, she reminds the audience of the Proserpina myth, the abduction of Ceres' daughter: "O Proserpina, / For the flow'rs now, that, frighted, thou let'st fall / From Dis's waggon!" (4. 4. 116–18). François

Laroque points out that the Perdita-Hermione connection parallels the myth of Proserpina and Ceres, the theme of which is "fertility" as well as "estrangement between mother and daughter" ("Pagan Ritual" 26). Moreover, Hermione's resurrection, brought by Leontes' sixteen-year repentance, is also applicable to the Christian context: the Resurrection of Christ and the forgiveness of sins. Laroque illustrates several parallels between the gospel and the play ("Pagan Ritual" 25–33). It is recorded that *The Winter's Tale* was performed at court on Easter Tuesday in 1618. Out of seven recorded performances for Eastertide, six are closely relevant to the resurrection theme (Hassel 140–55). Thus, the theme of death/rebirth resonates in the play both in a pagan ritual and a Christian liturgical context.

If the festive elements are the vehicles of the idea of death/rebirth, the bear chasing Antigonus is all the more puzzling. The device seems too bizarre for one to signify the arrival of the lively season. Michael Bristol observes that the bear on the stage was artificial, having manifold symbolic functions directly related to observances of Carnival. According to Bristol:

> A bear, usually a man dressed in furs or animal skins, appears in a variety of popular festive observances, occasionally during the Christmas season but more often in the later stages of the winter cycle. A straw bear appears as part of the observances of Plough Monday in parts of England. In France a bear or bear chase is associated with the feast of Candlemas, 2 February, and the feast of St. Blaise, 3 February, the earliest possible date for Shrove Tuesday. The bear also participates in Shrovetide observances in Bohemia.
>
> ("Search" 159)

If the audience were familiar with these customs, the actor in bearskin chasing Antigonus may have been directly associated with the festivities. Bristol further discusses: "the first half of the play is dominated by the temporal forms of Christmastide" because "hospitality is dominant preoccupation of scenes 1 and 2" (154). "In the second half of the play, the symbolism of Midsummer is augmented by the practical temporality of rural life" (154). Then, Bristol regards the bear's appearance in Act 3, Scene 3 as a symbolic representation of Carnival between Christmastide and Lent. If so, Antigonus' final speech, "This is the chase; / I am gone for ever" (3. 3. 57–58), is nothing more than a joke in the festive context.

Bristol further notices that the carnival period was exceptionally short in the years when the original performance was probably held:

> In the years 1610 and 1611, when this play was initially performed, Shrove Tuesday fell on or very near its earliest possible date of 3 February. In 1611 Ash Wednesday fell on 4 February, which meant that the gap between Christmastide and Lent was limited to a single day, that is, Shrove Tuesday. In those years Candlemas would have been linked very directly to pre-Lenten observances of Shrovetide. But this early date for Ash Wednesday would compress the permissible time for carnivalesque observances to almost nothing.
> ("Search" 161)

Then, Bristol concludes that "the condensation amounting to a complete omission of time for carnival is reflected in the structure of *The Winter's Tale*."

Bristol's idea of connecting the bear's hasty appearance and the calendar of 1610 and 1611 seems far-fetched. However, his general view that the play reflects offstage reality is worth noting. Critics have paid much attention to Autolycus, who has many parallels with rogues, peddlers, jugglers, and ballad mongers of cotemporary England (Salgado 135–50), while the Shepherd and the Clown have not been focus of attention. However, the comic conversation between the Shepherd and the Clown is full of social satire on offstage reality.

First, in the scene immediately after the bear's exit, they pick up a forlorn baby who is in rich attire, and also find a bundle, in which gold is wrapped, left beside her:

> *Shep.* [...] Here's a sight for thee; look thee, a bearing-cloth for a squire's child! Look thee here, take up, take up, boy; open't. So, let's see — it was told me I should be rich by the fairies. This is some changeling; open't; what's within, boy?
> *Clo.* You're a [made] old man; if the sins of your youth are forgiven you, you're well to live. Gold, all gold!
> *Shep.* This is fairy gold, boy, and 'twill prove so. Up with't, keep it close. Home, home, the next way. We are lucky, boy, and to be so still requires nothing but secrecy. Let my sheep go. Come, good boy, the next way home.
> (3. 3. 114–27)

Finding the treasure, the Shepherd mentions that they are "lucky" because it is a gift from "fairies." They gratefully bring the gold to their house and keep their wealth from anyone's notice. This is a seemingly innocent story of the poor Shepherd and his son, who are blessed by an unexpected fortune. However, the episode in *Pandosto* is slightly different from this.

In *Pandosto*, the Shepherd is torn between joy at finding the gold and fear of being noticed by his neighbors. He is in a dilemma whether to bring the child to his house, because he does not actually want to. However, he finally decides to foster the child, because he is in dire need and wants the gold.

> Taking therefore the Chylde in his armes, as he foulded the mantle together, the better to defend it from colde, there fell downe at his foote a very faire and riche purse, wherein he

founde a great summe of golde: which sight so revived the shepheards spirits, as he was greatly ravished with joy, and daunted with feare: Joyfull to see such a summe in his power, and fearefull if it should be knowne, that it might breede his further daunger. Necessitie wisht him at the least, to retaine the Golde, though he would not keepe the childe: the simplicity of his conscience scared him from such deceiptfull briberie. [...] So that he was resolved in himselfe to foster the child, and with the summe to relieve his want: resting thus resolute in this point he left seeking of his sheepe, and as covertly, and secretly as he coulde, went by a by way to his house, least any of his neighbours should perceave his carriage:

(Bullough 8: 174)

In *The Winter's Tale*, the Shepherd's psychological conflict is completely shaved off to make the scene comic. Without hesitation, the Shepherd brings the baby and the gold to his house, cautiously concealing them from their neighbors. Immediately after his exit, Time, the Chorus, enters to epitomize the actions of sixteen years. In the first scene after a gap of sixteen years, it is revealed that the Shepherd has become incredibly wealthy and also has a beautiful daughter:

> *Pol.* [...] from whom I have
> this intelligence, that he is seldom from the house of a
> most homely shepherd, a man, they say, that from very
> nothing, and beyond the imagination of his neighbors, is
> grown into an unspeakable estate.
> *Cam.* I have heard, sir, of such a man, who hath a
> daughter of most rare note. The report of her is
> extended more than can be thought to begin from such
> a cottage.
>
> (4. 2. 36–44)

The Shepherd's great estate is further highlighted in the next scene, where the Clown calculates the cash income from their sheep-shearing; the Shepherd is a capitalist who keeps as many as fifteen hundred sheep:

> *Clo.* Let me see: every 'leven wether tods, every
> tod yields pound and odd shilling; fifteen hundred
> shorn, what comes the wool to?
> (4. 3. 32–34)

The Shepherd's high living is also proved by the Clown's shopping list, in which expensive foodstuffs are enumerated.

> *Clo.* I cannot do't without compters. Let me see:
> what am I to buy for our sheep-shearing feast? Three
> pound of sugar, five pound of currants, rice - what will
> this sister of mine do with rice? But my father hath
> made her mistress of the feast, and she lays it on.
> She hath made me four and twenty nosegays for the
> shearers (three-man song-men all, and very good ones),
> but they are most of them means and bases; but one
> Puritan amongst them, and he sings psalms to horn-
> pipes. I must have saffron to color the warden
> pies; mace; dates, none – that's out of my note; nut-
> megs, seven; a race or two of ginger, but that I may
> beg; four pounds of pruins, and as many of raisins o'
> th' sun.
> (4. 3. 36–49)

Sugar, currants and rice are probably used for a rice pudding, which is served at the sheep-shearing dinner. Above all, rice was a very rare commodity only available in a market economy (Bristol "Search" 165). Spices such as saffron were obviously luxurious ingredients. In *Questions of Profitable and Pleasant Concernings* (1594), the excessive cost of a sheep-shearing feast is denounced: "If it be a sheep-shearing feast, maister Baily can entertain you with his bill of reckonings to his Maister, of three sheapheards wages, spent on fresh cates, besides spices and Saffron pottage" (4). The Shepherd's episode in *The Winter's Tale*, which is a seemingly innocent tale, may have symbolically reflected the upward mobility of contemporary capitalist society.

The bear-eaten Antigonus, narrated by the Clown, deserves further consideration. Having witnessed Antigonus' end, the Clown says: "he cried to me for help, and said his name was / Antigonus, a nobleman" (3. 3. 96–97). The Clown further reports that "the bear half din'd on the gentleman. He's at it now" (3. 3. 106). The Clown's speech is obviously a caricature of a perishing "gentleman." On the other hand, the Shepherd becomes an upstart "gentleman" (Palmer 291) because of the baby and the gold left by Antigonus. The bear scene is a turning point not only in dramatic structure but also in the Shepherd's social status.

As discussed in the previous chapter, *The Seven Champions of Christendom* includes many parodies of Shakespeare's late plays. The comic dialogue between the Clown and the Shepherd is inserted immediately after the Chorus summarizes the actions of seven years. This is a parody of the two sequential scenes of *The Winter's Tale*. Moreover, in *The Seven Champions*, the Clown laments his downward fall of status after the seven-year interval, showing nostalgia for the plentiful provisions of yore. This is also the travesty of the Shepherd's great success in *The Winter's Tale*. The parody intended in *The Seven Champions* clearly suggests that the mobility of social classes, exemplified by the Shepherd's transformation before and after the Time Chorus, was one of the central concerns of the contemporary audience.

The circulation of money is recognizable even in the pastoral scene. Simon Forman left a note about the performance of *The Winter's Tale* at the Globe on 15 may 1611, and his description was mostly about Autolycus who "haunts wakes, fairs, and bear-baitings" (4. 3. 102) to "cut most of their festival / purses" (4. 4. 614–15). Forman wrote down a warning against feigned beggars: "Beware of trusting feined beggars of fawninge fellouss" (Chambers *Elizabethan* 2: 341). This indicates that the presence of rogues at a festival was common in reality (Carroll 168–71). In the sheep-shearing, Autolycus appears as a peddler, who sells various commodities including ballads. He sings: "Come to the pedlar, / Money's a meddler" (4. 4. 321–22). The peddler is regarded as an embodiment of the circulation of money (Bristol "Search" 163; Carroll 171–72; Woodbridge 143–70). The pastoral ritual, signifying a lifecycle of death/rebirth, is juxtaposed with the fluidity of urban economy.

In the sheep-shearing, the issue of social class is repeatedly questioned by the characters in disguise. The innocent love between Florizel and Perdita is made problematic by their different births. Florizel's noble identity is concealed by his "swain's" garment, while Perdita, the queen of the feast, is dressed like a goddess:

> *Per.* Sir, my gracious lord,
> To chide at your extremes it not becomes me.
> O, pardon, that I name them! Your high self,
> The gracious mark o' th' land, you have obscur'd
> With a swain's wearing, and me, poor lowly maid,
> Most goddess-like prank'd up. But that our feasts
> In every mess have folly, and the feeders
> Digest['t] with a custom, I should blush
> To see you so attir'd — sworn, I think,
> To show myself a glass.
>
> (4. 4. 5–14)

Florizel's father, Polixenes, and his subject, Camillo, are also in disguise, attending the feast to investigate Florizel's secret love with the Shepherd's daughter. Not knowing the truth that Florizel is princely born, the Shepherd says in front of his guests: "I give my daughter to him [Florizel], and will make / Her portion equal his" (4. 4. 385–86).

As Perdita says, disguise is nothing but a traditional festive entertainment. However, in *The Winter's Tale*, garments and apparel are particularly important, serving as a vehicle of one's shifting identity (Carroll 173–74). For example, Autolycus first appears in rags, pretending to be a victim attacked by a rogue. He says: "That's the rogue / that put me into this apparel" (4. 3. 103–104). The Clown is deceived by Autolycus' appearance. Autolycus then appears in the likeness of a peddler. Finally, he transforms into a courtier by exchanging his apparel with Florizel, the prince of Bohemia. Camillo says to Autolycus: "for the outside of thy poverty we must / make an exchange" (4. 4. 632–33).

In early modern society, clothing was a kind of status symbol, representing one's gender, profession and wealth. Thus, neither cross-dressing nor "social" cross-dressing was approved, because they were considered as transgressions against social boundaries (Kastan 104–06; Howard 36–44). In particular, extravagant costume was criticized as an expression of one's wicked pride. Philip Stubbes denounces luxurious apparel in *The Anatomie of Abuses* from a puritanical perspective (90–131). In Robert Greene's *A Quip for an Vpstart Courtier* (1592), velvet-breeches and cloth-breeches represent two different social ranks: the new gentry and the ancient nobility. In short, apparel directly reflected one's wealth and rank.

Luxurious clothes were also prohibited by law. Under the reign of Elizabeth, Sumptuary Laws of Apparel were issued ten times between 1559 and 1588 (Hughes 2: 136–38; 187–203; 278–83; 381–86; 417; 454–62; 3: 3–8). However, the repeated proclamations ironically suggest that the legislation did not work, probably because the violation was too frequent. First, the Sumptuary Laws were largely applied to the middle and lower classes who could afford to buy luxurious commodities, including clothes. Since upward mobility was a remarkable phenomenon in the capitalistic economy, violation of the law may have been inevitable. Secondly, the Sumptuary Laws had economic motives: encouraging home industries, such as the English wool trade, and cutting down the market for imported luxurious fabrics (Kastan 104). However, London was the foremost center of cloth trade, particularly in the late sixteenth century. People's fashion dramatically changed in texture, shape and color, and cosmopolitan clothing prevailed (Schneider 109–27). In 1604, the Sumptuary Law was finally repealed.

Barnabee Rych's *The Honestie of This Age* (1614) suggests that his contemporaries were highly concerned with their attire. Rych laments that women wear fashionable clothes even when they go to church:

> You shall see some women goe so attyred to the Church, that I am ashamed to tell it out aloud, but harke in your eare, I will speake it softly, fitter in good faith, to furnish A.B.H. then to presse into the House of God: they are so be paynted so be periwigd, so be poudered, so be perfumed, so bee starched, so be laced, and so bee imbrodered, that I cannot tell what mentall virtues they may haue that they do keepe inwardly to themselues, but I am sure, to the outward show, it is a hard matter in the church it selfe to distinguish between a good woman, and a bad.
>
> (15)

Rych insists that such showy fashion comes from the "monstrous sin of pride." However, he concludes: "it is now growne into a fashion, and it is become so general, that it is but in vaine for any man to speake against it" (47). Rych's description clearly suggests that sumptuous fashion was prevailing, and that "social" cross-dressing was common off stage.

Against this background, actors' disguise may have been particularly amusing for the fashion-conscious audience. The theater was a place where a man of lower rank could transform himself into a nobleman, a woman or even a king by wearing their distinctive apparel, as well as by imitating their language and gestures. Jean Howard observes that "the theater was the place where such transgressions were literally institutionalized" and "their practices encouraged parallel transgressions in their audiences" (34). David Scott Kastan similarly argues that the social cross-dressing in the theater was "an unmistakable sign of the vulnerability of the traditional culture of status to the transformative energies of capitalistic practice" (107). However, if we note a metaphorical function in actors' clothes as well as their speeches, the visual effect of the clothes may become more allegorical than a direct reflection of offstage reality (Ozawa 25–38).

In *The Winter's Tale*, Autolycus refers to his rich garments, pretending to be a courtier:

> *Aut.* Whether it like me or no, I am a courtier.
> Seest thou not the air of the court in these enfold-
> ings? Hath not my gait in it the measure of the court?
> Receives not thy nose court-odor from me? Reflect I
> not on thy baseness court-contempt?
>
> (4. 4. 730–34)

Autolycus' unsophisticated language is comically contrasted with his rich garments, and his counterfeit identity is all the more exaggerated. The Shepherd comments on Autolycus' unbecoming clothes:

> *Clo.* This cannot be but a great courtier.
> *Shep.* His garments are rich, but he wears them
> not handsomely.
> *Clo.* He seems to be the more noble in being
> fantastical. A great man, I'll warrant; I know by the
> picking on 's teeth.
>
> (4. 4. 748–53)

Similarly, in Act 5, Scene 2, the Shepherd and the Clown appear in rich garments, after they were recognized as Perdita's stepfather and brother-in-law. The following conversation is extremely comic as they discuss whether they are "gentlemen born":

> *Shep.* Come, boy, I am past moe children, but thy
> sons and daughters will be all gentlemen born.

> *Clo.* You are well met, sir. You denied to fight
> with me this other day, because I was no gentleman
> born. See you these clothes? Say you see them
> not and think me still no gentleman born. You were
> best say these robes are not gentlemen born. Give me
> the lie, do; and try whether I am not now a gentleman
> born.
> *Aut.* I know you are now, sir, a gentleman born.
> *Clo.* Ay, and have been so any time these four
> hours.
> *Shep.* And so have I, boy.
> *Clo.* So you have. But I was a gentleman born
> before my father; for the King's son took me by
> the hand, and call'd me brother; and then the two kings
> call'd my father brother ; and then Prince, my
> brother, and the Princess, my sister, call'd my father
> father; and so we wept; and there was the first gentle-
> man-like tears that ever we shed.
> (5. 2. 126–45)

The Shepherd first obtained a great estate by finding a deserted baby and gold, and finally becomes a "gentleman born" because his stepdaughter is identified as a Sicilian princess. The Shepherd's subplot ends happily with his obtainment of wealth and status. However, the comic conversation quoted above suggests that his garment/status is obviously unbecoming. It is satirically questioned whether the status of a gentleman matches the birth of the commonalty.

On the other hand, in the main plot, Perdita proves that noble birth is never counterfeit. In the sheep-shearing, Polixenes says to Camillo: Perdita is "too noble for this place" (4. 4. 159). Florizel also says to Camillo: "She [Perdita]'s as forward of her breeding as / She is i' th' rear 'our birth" (4. 4. 580–81). The happy marriage between Florizel and Perdita is brought by the revelation of Perdita's royal identity. However, in the end,

Hermione's wondrous resurrection from Julio Romano's lifelike sculpture makes the question an open one. "This is an art / Which does mend Nature — change it rather; but / The art itself is Nature" (4. 4. 95–97). Thus, embracing the matter of birth and breeding, the artificial tale is itself fused with the natural offstage world.

Conclusion

Shakespeare's Romances have been considered to form a distinctive group in the history of early modern drama. They have common themes such as death/rebirth, family reunion and a happy marriage. They are also characterized by a theatrical emphasis on spectacle and music, and a wish-fulfillment happy ending. Critics have paid much attention to their unique character, rather than finding their similarities with other contemporary romances. However, while the King's Men performed Shakespeare's Romances at the Globe, the Queen's Men competed with them by acting out pseudo-historical or ancient folkloric romances such as *The Ages and The Seven Champions of Christendom* at the Red Bull. At the Hope, Ben Jonson's *Bartholomew Fair* was played in rivalry with the romance plays. Against this background around 1610, Shakespeare's Romances cannot have been isolated from the contemporary trend.

In this dissertation, I examined seven festive romances including Shakespeare's late plays. All of them are reminiscent of the folk festive tradition and have characteristics of wish-fulfillment fantasy, in which nostalgia for ancient hospitality and contemporary mobile society is overtly or covertly reflected. In each play, topical allusions, fused into the ancient fictional settings, serve to juxtapose the past and the present. In *The Old Wives Tale*, the framework of Madge's story-telling represents the generous hospitality of the good old days, while a series of inset stories are a satire on decaying hospitality and the harsh reality of contemporary poor relief in parish communities. In *Summer's Last Will and Testament*, the plot consists of the accounts given by the festive characters, who each represent their own social rank. In *George a Greene*, which has been grouped into Robin Hood plays, elevation of the commonalty is skillfully incorporated into the old legend of Pinder of Wakefield.

It is generally agreed that the successful revival of *Mucedorus* created a vogue for romance and gave Shakespeare some ideas for his late plays. In fact, there are similarities between *Mucedorus* and Shakespeare's Romances: a dichotomy between the civilized world and the innocence of nature, identity issues of a disguised prince or princess, a happy ending with reunion and marriage. In comparison with Shakespeare's Romances, however, *Mucedorus* is obviously less sophisticated and has not drawn scholarly attention. However, the play was very popular in the Elizabethan and Stuart periods, as the text was printed at least 17 times between 1598 and 1668. The play undoubtedly reflects the taste of contemporary audiences. In this dissertation, Mucedorus is a key to understanding Shakespeare's Romances.

The Seven Champions is also a minor play, which has never been the focus of scholarly attention. However, the play is full of allusive comments on Shakespeare's Romances. The parody of *The Winter's Tale* is evident in the comic dialogue between the Clown and the Shepherd, which immediately follows the Chorus in *The Seven Champions*, and vice versa in *The Winter's Tale*. *The Seven Champions* was probably written shortly after the great success of Shakespeare's Romances. In *Mucedorus* and *The Seven Champions*, the Clown's satiric allusions to the mobile social classes are mixed into the folkloric romance.

In Shakespeare's Romances, the hospitality issue and circulation of money are allegorically presented. In *Pericles*, Gower's chorus is deliberately archaic, based on the ancient tale which was widely circulated during the Medieval and the Renaissance period. Gower refers to the two specific festive occasions, "ember-eves" and "holy-ales," both of which are directly relevant to the hospitality issue. In the drama, hospitality is symbolically presented before and after Gower's second Chorus. Social satires are also recognizable in the brothel scenes, in which wealthy gentlemen's dishonesty is caricatured. However, the satires on the off-stage reality are tactfully fused into Gower's moralizing tale without giving any offense.

Conclusion

In The *Winter's Tale*, the sheep-shearing directly reflects decaying hospitality and circulation of money. The Shepherd, who obtains wealth and status by finding a deserted baby, finally becomes a gentleman when his stepdaughter is identified as a Sicilian princess. Then garments and apparel serve as a vehicle of one's shifting identity. Shepherd's unsophisticated language is comically contrasted with his rich garments, and his counterfeit identity is all the more exaggerated. Sumptuary Law of Apparel was finally repealed in 1604 off stage. In the play, it is satirically questioned whether the status of a gentleman matches the birth of the commonalty.

Romances are most unique in their techniques to break illusion and detach the audience's attention from the action of the drama. Such a device is to give the audience a larger collective vision of the world. In other words, the fiction created on the stage serves as a mirror of offstage reality. In the romance plays analyzed in this dissertation, festive elements are predominant. However, it has been clear that they are more relevant to the socioeconomic context than the festivity itself because they are also the artifacts of the early modern socio-economic transitional period.

Notes

1. According to Ronald Hutton's extensive research, church ales are recorded in 47 parishes, plough Monday gatherings are 6, Hocktide collections are 9, and the records of parish drama are numerous. In addition to these, the payments for minstrels, fools, Morris dancers, and Robin Hood are also found (113–15).

2. According to the ongoing achievement of the *Records of Early English Drama*, it has become clear that the degree of suppressing festivals varied from region to region. There are records to show that festivals were held even after the 17th century (Sisson *Lost Plays* 162–77; Stoke "The Wells Cordwainers Show," "The Wells Shows of 1607"; Sale "Slanderous Aesthetics"; Bennett "Conviviality and Charity" 26–28; Greenfield "Regional").

3. In "The Argument of Comedy" (1948), Frye argues that Elizabethan plays come "not from the Mysteries or the Moralities or the interludes, but from a fourth dramatic tradition" like St George plays and mummers' plays. Frye calls the folk ritual "the drama of the green world," and says that "its theme is once again the triumph of life over the waste land, the death and revival of the year impersonated by figures still human and once divine as well" (321). In his *Anatomy of Criticism* (1957), Frye only suggests that there is a similarity between the archetypal rites of Saturnalia and comic forms, in which heroes temporarily rebel against existing orders and finally reconcile with them (171).

4. Historians often suggest that festive inversions worked not only as a safety valve but were actually also dangerous. For example, Keith Thomas illustrates some cases where inversion games developed into apprentice riots and barring–out in school ("Rule and Misrule" 3–35). From a wider perspective, Peter Burke discusses the violent aspects of carnival in his *Popular Culture in Early Modern Europe* (199–204).

5. The quotations from *The Kalends of December* refer to Statius.

6. The definition of "hospitality" changed from the Middle Ages to the end of the 17th century. In the later Middle Ages, "hospitality" was linked to

clerical beneficence and included charitable giving to the poor. However, the idea of "charity" itself also changed in the course of the 16th century, and finally hospitality came to mean something offered to the peer group or to neighbors, and charity meant alms to the needy (Heal *Hospitality* 1–22).

7. All of Shakespeare's texts refer to *The Riverside Shakespeare* edition.

8. All of the country house poems quoted refer to Fowler.

9. "In fact, were I not, with my task well-nigh done, about to furl my sails and making haste to turn my prow to land, perchance I might sing what careful tendance clothes rich gardens in flower, and might sing of Paestum whose rose beds bloom twice yearly, how the endive rejoices in drinking streams, the verdant banks in celery; how the cucumber, coiling through the grass, swells into a paunch… I saw an old Cilician, who occupied a few acres of unclaimed land, not rich enough for ploughing, nor fit for pasturage, nor suited to the vine. Even so, planting cabbages here and there among the brambles, and white lilies and vervain and fine-seeded poppies, in happiness he equalled the wealth of kings, and returning home late at night he used to load his table with an unbought banquet" (227).

10. "How well lived folk in olden days when Saturn was the king, before the earth was opened out for distant travel! …No house had doors; no stone was planted on the land to set fixed boundaries to men's estates. The very oaks gave honey; and with milky udders came the ewes unbidden to meet the carefree swain" (207).

11. "The dish you used to send me at Saturn's time, Sextilianus, you sent to your mistress, and the green dinner suit you gave her on the Kalends that take their name from Mars was bought out of *my* gown…The line does not seek its prey in the far-off sea, but the fish, watched from above, draws the string tossed from bed or couch" (vol. II p. 351–53).

12. All of the quotations from *The Old Wives Tale* refer to the edition by Hook.

13. Whitworth gives "a chart of stage appearances of characters" and shows the possibilities of doubling (56–57).

14. For the research on masks in the medieval theater, See Twycross and Carpenter; and Beadle.

15. For example, "Somerset Wassail" in *We Wish You A Merry Christmas*.

16. Marx points out that "The Grateful Dead" is very similar to the medieval romance, *Sir Amadice* (133–34).

17. Costumes of the mummer's plays vary from region to region. The many plates are included in Helm's *The English Mummers' Play*.

18. Posluszny's introduction in her Thomas Nashe's *Summer's Last Will and Testament: A Critical Modern-Spelling Edition* (1989) is based on Barber's view.

19. All of the quotations from *George a Greene* refer to the edition (1905) by Collins.

20. All of the quotations from *Mucedorus* refer to the edition (1976) by Russell A. Fraser and Norman C. Rabkin.

21. All of the quotations from *The Seven Champions of Christendom* refer to the edition (1637) by K.

22. All of the quotations from *Bartholomew Fair* refer to the edition by H. Percy and Evelyn Simpson.

Works Cited

Primary Sources

Adams, J. Q, ed. *Chief Pre-Shakespearean Dramas*. London: George G. Harrap.
B, O. *Questions of Profitable and Pleasant Concernings*. London, 1594. STC 1054.
Beaumont, Francis. *The Knight of the Burning Pestle*. Ed. Sheldon P. Zitner. Manchester: Manchester UP, 1984.
Binnie, Patricia, ed. *The Old Wives Tale*. Manchester: Manchester UP, 1980.
Boas, Frederick S, ed. *The Christmas Prince*. Oxford: Malone Society, 1923.
Brathwaite, Richard. *A Strappado for the Diuell. Epigrams and Satyres Alluding to the Time, with Diuers Measures of No Lesse Delight*. London, I. B, 1615. STC 3588.
Breton, Nicholas. *Fantastickes*. In *The Works in Verse and Prose of Nicholas Breton*. Ed. Alexander B. Grosart. Vol. 2. New York: AMS, 1966.
---. *A Merrie Dialoguve betwixt the Taker and Mistaker*. London, 1603. STC 3667.
Brooke, C. F. Tucker, ed. *The Shakespeare Apocrypha*. 1908 rpt. Oxford: Clarendon P, 1967.
Brookhouse, Christopher. *Sir Amadace and the Avowing of Arthur: Two Romances from the Ireland MS. Anglistica*. Vol. 15. Copenhagen: Rosenkilde and Bagger, 1968.
Bullough, Geoffrey. *Narrative and Dramatic Sources of Shakespeare*. Vol.6. 1966 rpt. London and New York: Routledge, 1996.
---. *Narrative and Dramatic Sources of Shakespeare*. Vol. 8. 1975 rpt. London and New York: Routledge, 1996.
Collins, J. Churton, ed. *A Pleasant Conceyted Comedie of George A Greene, The Pinner of Wakefield*. In *The Plays & Poems of Robert Greene*. Vol. 2. Oxford: Clarendon P, 1905.
Creigh, Geoffrey and Jane Belfield, eds. *The Cobler of Caunterburie and Tarltons Newes out of Purgatorie*. Leiden: E. J. Brill, 1987.
Dekker, Thomas. *A Strange Horse-Race*. In *The Non-Dramatic Works of Thomas Dekker*. Vol. 3. Ed. Alexander B. Grosart. New York: Russel & Russell,

1963.

---. *The Shoemaker's Holiday*. Eds. R. L. Smallwood and Stanley Wells. Manchester: Manchester UP, 1979.

Deloney, Thomas. *The Works of Thomas Deloney*. Ed. Francis Oscar Mann. Oxford: Clarendon P, 1912.

DelVecchio, Doreen and Antony Hammond, eds. *Pericles*. Cambridge: Cambridge UP, 1998.

Foakes, R. A, ed. *Henslowe's Diary*. 2nd ed. Cambridge: Cambridge UP, 2002.

Fowler, Alastair, ed. *The Country House Poem: A Cabinet of Seventeenth-Century Estate Poems and Related Items*. Edinburgh: Edinburgh UP, 1994.

Gassner, John, ed. *Medieval and Tudor Drama*. 1963 rpt. New York: Applause Books, 1987.

Gossett, Suzanne, ed. *Pericles*. Arden Shakespeare, 2004.

Great Frost, The. In *Social England Illustrated. A Collection of XVIIth Century Tracts*. Ed. Andrew Lang. Edinburgh: Archibald Constable, 1903.

Graigie, O. B. E. James, ed. *Minor Prose Works of King James VI and I: Daemonologie, The Trve Lawe of Free Monarchies, A Counterblaste to Tobacco, A Declaration of Sports*. Edinburgh: Scottish Text Society, 1982.

Greene, Robert. *A Quip for an Vpstart Courtier: or, A Quaint Dispute betvveen Veluet Breeches and Cloth-breeches*. In *The Life and Complete Works in Prose and Verse of Robert Greene*. Vol. 11. Ed. Alexander B. Grosart. New York: Russell & Russell, 1964.

Hall, Joseph. *The Poems of Joseph Hall*. Ed. Arnold Davenport. 1949 rpt. Liverpool: Liverpool UP, 1969.

Harrison, C. J. *The Elizabethan Parish: A Collection of Documents*. Keele: Keele UP, 2001.

Herrick, Robert. *The Poetical Works of Robert Herrick*. Ed. F. W. Moorman. With a prefatory note by Percy Simpson. 1921 rpt. London: Oxford UP, 1936.

Heywood, Thomas. *The Dramatic Works of Thomas Heywood: Now First Collected with Illustrative Notes and a Memoir of the Author*. Vol. 2. 1874 rpt. New York: Russell & Russell, 1964.

Hook, Frank S, ed. *The Old Wives Tale*. In *The Dramatic Works of George Peele*. Vol. 3. New Haven: Yale UP, 1970.

Hughes, Paul L. and James F. Larkin, eds. *Tudor Royal Proclamations*. 3 Vols. New Haven: Yale UP, 1969.

Jacobs, Joseph, ed. *English Fairy Tales*. rpt. 1890. London: Everyman's Library, 1993.

Johnson, Richard. *The Seven Champions of Christendom* (1596/7). Ed. Jeniffer Fellows. Aldershot: Ashgate, 2003.

---. *A Crwone-Garland of Govlden Roses: Gathered out of Englands Royall Garden*. London, 1612. STC 14672.

Jupin, Arvin H, ed. *A Contextual Study and Modern-Spelling Edition of Mucedorus*. The Renaissance Imagination Volume 29. New York: Garland,1987.
Juvenal. *Satires*. In *Juvenal and Persius*. Loeb Classical Library. Trans. G. G. Ramsay. 1918 rpt. Cambridge, Mass.: Harvard UP, 1999.
K, J. *The Seven Champions of Christendome. Acted at the Cocke-pit, and at the Red-Bull in St. Johns Streete, with a Generall Liking, And Never Printed till this Yeare 1638*. London, 1638. STC 15014.
Knight, Stephen and Thomas Ohlgren, eds. *Robin Hood and Other Outlaw Tales*. 2nd ed. TEAMS Middle English Texts Series. Kalamazoo: Medieval Institute Publications, 2000.
Larkin, James F. and Paul L. Hughes, eds. *Stuart Royal Proclamations. Volume I: Royal Proclamations of King James I 1603–1625*. Oxford: Clarendon P, 1973.
---, ed. *Stuart Royal Proclamations. Volume II: Royal Proclamations of King Charles I 1625–1646*. Oxford: Clarendon P, 1983.
Look About You. Ed. W. W. Greg. 1913 rpt. New York: AMS, 1985.
Lucian. *Saturnalia*. In *Lucian*. Vol. 6: Loeb Classical Library. Trans. K. Kilburn. Cambridge, Mass.: Harvard UP, 1959.
Manley, John Matthews, ed. *Specimens of the Pre-Shakespearean Drama*. 1897 rpt. New York: Biblo and Tannen, 1967.
Manley, Lawrence, ed. *London in the Age of Shakespeare: An Anthology*. London & Sydney: Croom Helm, 1986.
Martial. *Epigrams*. 3 vols. Loeb Classical Library. Ed. and Trans. D. R. Shackleton Bailey. Cambridge, Mass.: Harvard UP, 1993.
McIlwain, Charles Howard, ed. *The Political Works of James I*. Harvard: Harvard UP, 1918.
Merry Knack to Know a Knave, A. In *A Select Collection of Old English Plays*. 4th ed. Vols.6 & 7. Ed. W. Carew Hazlitt. 1744 rpt. New York: Benjamin Blom, 1964.
Middleton, Thomas. *A Chaste Maid in Cheapside*. Ed. R. B. Parker. London: Methuen, 1969.
Most Pleasant Comedie of Mucedorus the Kings Sonne of Valentia and Amadine the Kings Daughter of Arragon. with the Merie Conceites of Mouse. London, 1610. STC 18232.
Mucedorus 1598. Ed. John S. Farmer. 1910 rpt. New York: AMS, 1970.
Mucedorus. In *Drama of the English Renaissance*. Vol.1: The Tudor Period. Eds. Russell A. Fraser and Norman Rabkin. New Jersey: Prentice-Hall, 1976.
Munday, Anthony. *The Downfall of Robert Earl of Huntington*. In *A Select Collection of Old English Plays*. 4th ed. Vol. 8 & 9. Ed. W. Carew Hazlitt. 1744 rpt. New York: Benjamin Blom, 1964.
---. *The Death of Robert Earl of Huntington*. In *A Select Collection of Old English*

Plays. 4th ed. Vol. 8 & 9. Ed. W. Carew Hazlitt. 1744 rpt. New York: Benjamin Blom, 1964.

Nashe, Thomas. *A Pleasant Comedie, Called Summers Last Will and Testament.* In *The Works of Thomas Nashe.* Vol. 3. Ed. Ronald B. McKerrow. Oxford: Basil Blackwell, 1966.

Orgel, Stephen, ed. *The Winter's Tale.* Oxford: Oxford UP, 1996.

Paul, George. *The Life of John Whitgift, Archbishop of Canterbury in the Times of Queen Elizabeth and King James I.* London, 1612. STC 19484.

Peele, George. *The Old Wives Tale.* In *The Dramatic Works of George Peele.* Vol. 3. Ed. Frank S. Hook. New Haven: Yale UP, 1970.

---. *Edward I.* In *The Dramatic Works of George Peele.* Vol. 2. Ed. Frank S. Hook. New Haven: Yale UP, 1961.

Percy, Herford C. H. and Evelyn Simpson, eds. *Bartholomew Fair.* In *Ben Jonson* Vol. 6. Oxford: Clarendon P, 1938.

Percy, Thomas, ed. *The Percy Folio of Old English Ballads and Romances.* Vol. 1. London: De La More Press, 1905.

---. *Reliques of Ancient English Poetry.* Vol. 3. 1886 rpt. New York: Dover Publications, 1966.

Petronius. *Satyricon.* Trans. W. H. D. Rouse. 1913 rpt. Cambridge, Mass.: Harvard UP, 1997.

Pleasant Satyre or Poesie, A: Wherein is Discouered the Catholicon of Spayne, and the Chiefe Leaders of the League. London, 1595. STC 154989.

Poor Robins Hue and Cry After Good House-Keeping. Or, a Dialogue Betwixt Good House-Keeping, Christmas, and Pride. London, 1687. STC 2884A.

Posluszny, Patricia, ed. *Summer's Last Will and Testament: A Critical Modern-spelling Edition.* New York: Peter Lang, 1989.

Ritson, Joseph. *Robin Hood: A Collection of All the Ancient Poems, Songs and Ballads, Now Extant, Relative to that Celebrated English Outlaw.* 2 vols. 1887 rpt. London: Routledge / Thoemmes, 1997.

Rowe, John. *Tragi-Comedia.* Ed. Arthur Freeman. New York: Garland, 1973.

Rowland, David, trans. *The Life of Lazarillo de Tormes.* Warminster: Aris & Phillips, 2000.

Rowley, William. *A Shoemaker, A Gentleman.* Ed. Trudi L. Darby. New York: Routledge, 2003.

Rych, Barnabee. *The Honestie of This Age: Proouing by Good Circumstance That the World Was Neuer Honest till Now.* London, 1614. STC 20986.

Shakespeare, William. *The Riverside Shakespeare.* 2nd ed. Eds. G. Blakemore Evans and J. J. M. Tobin. Boston: Houghton Mifflin, 1997.

---. *The Late, and Much Admired Play, Called Pericles, Prince of Tyre.* London, 1609. STC 22334.

Statius. *Silvae.* Loeb Classical Library. Ed. and Trans. D. R. Shackleton Bailey.

Cambridge, Mass.: Harvard UP, 2003.
Stow, John. *A Survey of London Written in the Year 1598*. Ed. Antonia Fraser. 1994 rpt. London: Sutton Publishing, 1999.
Stubbes, Philip. *Anatomie of Abuses*. Ed. Margaret Jane Kidnie. Medieval and Renaissance Texts and Studies, Vol. 245. Arizona: Arizona State UP, 2002.
Thomas, William J, ed. *Early English Prose Romances*. Vol.2. London: Nattali and Bond, 1858.
Tibullus. In *Catullus Tibullus and Pervigilium Veneris*. Loeb Classical Library. Trans. J. P. Postgate. 1913 rep. Cambridge, Mass.: Harvard UP, 1956.
Tusser, Thomas. *Five Hundred Points of Good Husbandry*. Ed. James Tregaskis. With an Introduction by Geoffrey Grigson. Oxford: Oxford UP, 1984.
Virgil. *Georgics*. In Virgil I. Loeb Classical Library. Trans. G. P. Goold. Cambridge, Mass.: Harvard UP, 1999.
Warren, Roger, ed. *A Reconstructed Text of Pericles, Prince of Tyre by William Shakespeare and George Wilkins*. Oxford: Oxford UP, 2003.
We Wish You A Merry Christmas: 5 Secular Christmas Carols. Arranged by John Rutter. Chapel Hill: Hinshaw Music, 1985.
Whitworth, Charles, ed. *The Old Wives Tale*. 2nd ed. London: New Mermaids, 1996.
Wilkins, George. *The Painfull Aduentures of Pericles Prince of Tyre*. Ed. Kenneth Muir. Liverpool: U of Liverpool, 1953.
Wilson, Robert. *The Three Ladies of London*. In *A Select Collection of Old English Plays*. 4th ed. Vol.6 & 7. Ed. W. Carew Hazlitt. 1744 rpt. New York: Benjamin Blom, 1964.
---. *The Coblers Prophesie*(1594). Ed. A. C. Wood. Oxford: Malone Society Reprints, 1914.
---. *An Edition of Robert Wilson's* Three Ladies of London *and* Three Lords and Three Ladies of London. Ed. H. S. D. Mithal. New York: Garland, 1988.

Secondary Sources

Archer, Ian W. *The Pursuit of Stability: Social Relations in Elizabethan London*. Cambridge: Cambridge UP, 1991.
Archibald, Elizabeth. *Apollonius of Tyre: Medieval and Renaissance Themes and Variations*. Cambridge: D. S. Brewer, 1991.
Axton, Marie."Summer's Last Will and Testament: Revels' End." In *The Reign of Elizabeth I: Court and Culture in the Last Decade*. Ed. John Guy. Cambridge: Cambridge UP, 1995. 258–73.
Bakhtin, Mikhail. *Rabelais and His World*. Trans. Helene Iswolsky. 1968 rpt.

Bloomington: Indiana UP, 1984.
Barber, C. L. *Shakespeare's Festive Comedy: A Study of Dramatic Form and Its Relation to Social Custom*. Princeton: Princeton UP, 1959.
Barron, Caroline M. "Richard Whittington: The Man behind the Myth." In *Studies in London History*. Eds. A. E. J. Hollaender and William Kellaway. London: Hodder and Stoughton, 1969. 197–247.
Baskervill, Charles Read. "Dramatic Aspects of Medieval Folk Festivals in England." *Studies in Philology* 17 (1920): 19–87.
---. "Mummers' Wooing Plays in England." *Modern Philology*. Vol. 21, No. 3 (1924): 225–272.
---. *The Elizabethan Jig and Related Song Drama*. Chicago: U of Chicago P, 1929.
Beadle, Richard. "Masks, Mimes and Miracles: Medieval English Theatricality and Its Illusions." In *From Script to Stage in Early Modern England*. Eds. Peter Holland and Stephen Orgel. New York: Palgrave Macmillan, 2004. 32–42.
Beier, A. L. *The Problem of the Poor in Tudor and Early Stuart England*. London: Methuen, 1983.
---. *Masterless Men: The Vagrancy Problem in England 1560–1640*. London: Methuen, 1985.
Beier, A. L. and Roger Finlay, eds. *London 1500–1700: The Making of the Metropolis*. London and New York: Longman, 1986.
Bennett, Judith M. "Conviviality and Charity in Medieval and Early Modern England." *Past and Present* 134 (1992): 19–41.
Bergeron, David M. *English Civic Pageantry 1558–1642*. London: Edward Arnold, 1971.
Billington, Sandra. *Mock Kings in Medieval Society and Renaissance Drama*. Oxford: Clarendon P, 1991.
Bonahue, Jr. Edward T. "Heywood, the Citizen Hero, and the History of Dick Whittington." *English Language Notes* 36 (1999): 33–41.
Bristol, Michael D. *Carnival and Theater: Plebeian Culture and the Structure of Authority in Renaissance England*. New York: Methuen, 1985.
---. "In Search of the Bear: Spatiotemporal Form and the Heterogeneity of Economies in *The Winter's Tale*." *Shakespeare Quarterly* 42 (1991): 145–67.
Burke, Peter. "Popular Culture in Seventeenth-Century London." *The London Journal* 3 (1977): 141–62.
---. *Popular Culture in Early Modern Europe*. 1978 rpt. Aldershot: Scholar Press, 1994.
Camp, Charles W. *The Artisan in Elizabethan Literature*. 1924 rpt. New York: Octagon Books, 1972.
Campbell, Mildred. *The English Yeoman: Under Elizabeth and the Early Stuarts*. London: Merlin Press, 1960.

Carroll, William C. *Fat King, Lean Beggar: Representations of Poverty in the Age of Shakespeare*. Ithaca and London: Cornell UP, 1996.
Chambers, E. K. *The Mediaeval Stage*. 2 vols. Oxford : Oxford UP, 1903.
---. *The Elizabethan Stage*. 4 vols. 1923 rpt. Oxford: Clarendon P, 1974.
---. *The English Folk Play*. 1933 rpt. Oxford: Clarendon P, 1969.
Clark, Peter. *English Provincial Society from the Reformation to the Revolution: Religion, Politics and Society in Kent 1500–1640*. Hassocks: Harvest, 1977.
---. *The English Alehouse: A Social History 1200–1830*. London and New York: Longman, 1983.
Clubb, Louise G. "The Tragicomic Bear." *Comparative Literature Studies* 9 (1972): 17–30.
Cole, Howard C. *A Quest of Inquirie: Some Contexts of Tudor Literature*. New York: Bobbs-Merrill, 1973.
Colie, Rosalie L. *The Resources of Kind: Genre-Theory in the Renaissance*. Ed. Barbara K. Lewalski. Berkeley and Los Angeles: U of California P, 1973.
Cope, Jackson I. "Peele's *Old Wives' Tale*: Folk Stuff into Ritual Form." *English Literary History* 49 (1982): 326–38, rep. In his *Dramaturgy of the Daemonic: Studies in Antigeneric Theater from Ruzante to* Grimald. Baltimore: John Hopkins UP, 1984. 50–61.
Cox, John D. "Homely Matter and Multiple Plots in Peel's *Old Wives Tale*." *Texas Studies in Literature and Language* 20: 3 (1978): 330–46.
Cressy, David. *Bonfires and Bells: National Memory and the Protestant Calendar in Elizabethan and Stuart England*. Berkeley and Los Angeles: U of California P, 1989.
Davenport, Edwin. "The Representation of Robin Hood in Elizabethan Drama: *George a Greene* and *Edward I*." In *Playing Robin Hood: The Legend as Performance in Five Centuries*. Ed. Lois Potter. Newark: U of Delaware P, 1998. 45–62.
Davidson, Clifford. "'What hempen home-spuns have we swagg'ring here?': Amateur Actors in *A Midsummer Night's Dream* and the Coventry Civic Plays and Pageants." *Shakespeare Studies* 19 (1987): 87–99.
Doebler, John. "The Tone of George Peele's *The Old Wives Tale*." *English Studies* 53 (1972): 412–21.
Dubrow, Heather. "The Country-House Poem: A Study in Generic Development." *Genre* 12 (1979): 153–79.
Dynes, William R. "'London, Look On!.'" *Group for Early Modern Cultural Studies*. Pittsburgh: PA, 1996.
Evans, Robert C. *Ben Jonson and the Patronage*. Cranbury: Associated UP, 1989.
Felperin, Howard. *Shakespearean Romance*. Princeton: Princeton UP, 1972.
Frazer, James George. *The Golden Bough: A Study in Magic and Religion*. Ed. Robert Fraser. Oxford: Oxford UP, 1994.

Free, Mary G. "Audience within Audience in *The Old Wives Tale*." *Renaissance Papers* (1983): 53–61.

Freehafer, John. "Shakespeare's *Tempest* and *The Seven Champions*." *Studies in Philology* 66 (1969): 87–103.

Frost, David L. "'Mouldy Tales': The Context of Shakespeare's '*Cymbeline*.'" *Essays and Studies* (1986): 19–38.

Frye, Northrop. "The Argument of Comedy." In *Shakespeare's Comedies: An Anthology of Modern Criticism*. Ed. Laurence Lerner. London: Penguin, 1967. 315–25.

---. *Anatomy of Criticism: Four Essays*. Princeton: Princeton UP, 1957.

Geller, Sherri. "Commentary as Cover-Up: Criticizing Illiberal Patronage in Thomas Nashe's *Summer's Last Will and Testament*." *English Literary Renaissance* 25 (1995): 148–78.

Gerould, Gordon Hall. *The Grateful Dead: The History of a Folk Story*. Urbana and Chicago: U of Illinois P, 2000.

Goldsmith, Robert Hillis. "The Wild Man on the English Stage." *Modern Language Review* 53 (1958): 481–91.

Goring, Jeremy. *Godly Exercises or the Devil's Dance?: Puritanism and Popular Culture in Pre-Civil War England*. Inverness: Highland Printers, 1983.

Greenfield, Peter H. "Touring". In *A New History of Early English Drama*. Eds. John D. Cox and David Scott Kastan. New York: Columbia UP, 1997. 251–68.

---. "The Carnivalesque in the Robin Hood Games and King Ales of Southern England." In *Carnival and Carnivalesque: The Fool, the Reformer, the Wildman, and Others in Early Modern Theatre*. Eds. Konrad Eisenbichler and Wim Hüsken. Amsterdam: Atlanta, GA 1999. 19–28.

---. "Regional Performance in Shakespeare's Time." In *Region, Religion and Patronage: Lancastrian Shakespeare*. Eds. Richard Dutton, Alison Findlay and Richard Wilson. Manchester: Manchester UP, 2003. 243–51.

Griffiths, Paul. "The Structure of Prostitution in Elizabethan London." *Continuity and Change* 8:1 (1993): 39–63.

Gurr, Andrew. "The *Tempest*'s Tempest at Blackfriars." *Shakespeare Survey* 29 (1976): 91–102.

---. "The Bear, the Statue, and Hysteria in *The Winter's Tale*." *Shakespeare Quarterly* 34 (1983): 420–25.

---. "Money or Audiences: The Impact of Shakespeare's Globe." *Theatre Notebook* 42 (1988): 3–14.

---. "Playing in Amphitheatres and Playing in Hall Theatres." *The Elizabethan Theatre* XIII (1989): 47–62.

---. *The Shakespearian Playing Companies*. Oxford: Clarendon, 1996.

Hammond, N.G. L. and H.H. Scullard, eds. *The Oxford Classical Dictionary*.

1970. 2nd ed. Oxford: Clarendon P, 1992.
Hardman, Christopher. *The Winter's Tale*. London: Penguin Books, 1988.
Hassel, R. Chris, Jr. *Renaissance Drama & the English Church Year*. Lincoln: U of Nebraska P, 1979.
Hazlitt, W. Carew. *Faiths and Folklore of the British Isles: A Descriptive and Historical Dictionary*. Vol. 1. New York: Benjamin Blom, 1965.
---. *The Livery Companies of the City of London: their Origin, Character, Development, and Social and Political Importance*. 1892 rpt. New York: Benjamin Blom, 1969.
Heal, Felicity. *Of Prelates and Princes: A Study of the Economic and Social Position of the Tudor Episcopate*. Cambridge: Cambridge UP, 1980.
---. "The Archbishops of Canterbury and the Practice of Hospitality." *Journal of Ecclesiastical History* Vol. 33 No. 4 (1982): 544–63.
---. "The Idea of Hospitality in Early Modern England." *Past and Present*. No. 102 (1984): 66–93.
---. "The Crown, the Gentry and London: the Enforcement of Proclamation, 1596–1640." In *Law and Government under the Tudors*. Eds. Clair D. M. Cross, David Loades and J. J. Scarisbrick. Cambridge: Cambridge UP, 1988. 211–26.
---. *Hospitality in Early Modern England*. Oxford: Clarendon P, 1990.
---. *The Gentry in England and Wales 1500–1700*. Stanford: Stanford UP, 1994.
Helm, Alex. *The English Mummers' Play*. Suffolk and Totowa: D. S. Brewer and Rowman and Littlefield, 1981.
Hibbard, G. R. "The Country House Poem of the Seventeenth Century". *Journal of the Warburg and Courtauld Institutes* 19 (1956): 159–74.
---. *Thomas Nashe: A Critical Introduction*. London: Routledge and Kegan Paul, 1962.
Hill, Christopher. *Liberty Against the Law: Some Seventeenth-century Controversies*. London: Allen Lane (The Penguin Press), 1996.
Hill, Janet. *Stages and Playgoers: Form Guild Plays to Shakespeare*. Montreal: McGill Queen's UP, 2002.
Hindle, Steve. "A Sense of Place? Becoming and Belonging in the Rural Parish, 1550–1650." In *Communities in Early Modern England: Networks, Place, Rhetoric*. Eds. Alexandra Shepard and Phil Withington. Manchester: Manchester UP, 2000. 96–114.
---. "Dearth, Fasting and Alms: The Campaign for General Hospitality in Late Elizabethan England." *Past and Present* 172 (2001): 44–86.
Hoeniger, F. David. "Gower and Shakespeare in *Pericles*." *Shakespeare Quarterly* 33 (1982): 461–79.
Holland, Peter. "Theatre Without Drama: Reading *REED*." In *From Script to Stage in Early Modern England*. Eds. Peter Holland and Stephen Orgel. New

York: Palgrave Macmillan, 2004. 43–67.
Holt, J. C. *Robin Hood*. London: Thames and Hudson, 1982.
Howard, Jean E. *The Stage and Social Struggle in Early Modern England*. London and New York: Routledge, 1994.
Howatson, M. C, ed. *The Oxford Companion to Classical Literature*. 1937. 2nd ed. Oxford: Oxford UP, 1989.
Hutson, Lorna. *Thomas Nashe in Context*. Oxford: Clarendon P, 1989.
Hutton, Ronald. *The Rise and Fall of Merry England: The Ritual Year 1400–1700*. Oxford: Oxford UP, 1994.
Jackson, MacD. P. "Edward Archer's Ascription of 'Mucedorus' to Shakespeare." *Journal of the Australiasian Universities Language and Literature Association* 22 (1964): 233–48.
---. *Defining Shakespeare: Pericles as Test Case*. Oxford: Oxford UP, 2003.
James, E. O. *Seasonal Feasts and Festivals*. London: Thames and Hudson, 1961.
Jenkins, Harold. "Peele's 'Old Wive's Tale.'" *Modern Language Notes* 34 (1939): 177–85.
Johnston, Alexandra F. "Summer Festivals in the Thames Valley Counties." In *Custom, Culture and Community in the Later Middle Ages*. Ed. Thomas Pettitt. Odense: Odense UP, 1994. 37–56.
---. "'What Revels are in Hand?': Dramatic Activities Sponsored by the Parishes of the Thames Valley." In *English Parish Drama*. Eds. Alexandra F. Johnston & Wim Hüsken. Amsterdam: Atlanta, GA, 1996. 95–104.
Jones, Gareth. *History of the Law of Charity 1532–1827*. Cambridge: Cambridge UP, 1969.
Jordan, W. K. *Philanthropy in England 1480–1660: A Study of the Changing Pattern of English Social Aspirations*. 1959 rpt. Westport: Greenwood, 1978.
Kastan, David Scott. "Is There a Class in This (Shakespearean) Text?" *Renaissance Drama* 24 (1993): 101–21.
Kathman, David. "Grocers, Goldsmiths, and Drapers: Freemen and Apprentices in the Elizabethan Theater." *Shakespeare Quarterly* 55 (2004): 1–49.
Keenan, Siobhan. *Travelling Players in Shakespeare's England*. New York: Palgrave Macmillan, 2002.
Knights, L. C. *Drama & Society in the Age of Jonson*. London: Chatto & Windus, 1957.
Knight, Stephen. *Robin Hood: A Complete Study of the English Outlaw*. Oxford: Blackwell, 1994.
---. "Which Way to the Forest? Directions in Robin Hood Studies." In *Robin Hood in Popular Culture: Violence, Transgression, and Justice*. Ed. Thomas Hahn. Cambridge: D. S. Brewer, 2000. 111–28.
Laroque, François. "Pagan Ritual, Christian Liturgy, and Folk Customs in *The Winter's Tale*." *Cahiers Elisabéthains* 22 (1982):25–33.

---. *Shakespeare's Festive World: Elizabethan Seasonal Entertainment and the Professional Stage.* Cambridge: Cambridge UP, 1991.

Lawrence, W. J. "John Kirke, The Caroline Actor-Dramatist." *Studies in Philology* 21 (1924): 586–93.

Malcolmson, Robert W. *Popular Recreations in English Society 1700–1850.* Cambridge: Cambridge UP, 1973.

Manley, Lawrence. *Literature and Culture in Early Modern London.* Cambridge: Cambridge UP, 1995.

Marcus, Leah S. *The Politics of Mirth: Jonson, Herrick, Milton, Marvell, and the Defense of Old Holiday Pastimes.* Chicago: U of Chicago P, 1986.

---. "Politics and Pastoral: Writing the Court on the Countryside". In *Culture and Politics in Early Stuart England.* Eds. Kevin Sharpe and Peter Lake. London: Macmillan, 1994. 139–59.

Marx, Joan C. "'Soft, Who Have We Here?': The Dramatic Technique *of The Old Wives Tale*." *Renaissance Drama* 12 (1981): 117–43.

McBride, Kari Boyd. *Country House Discourse in Early Modern England: A Cultural Study of Landscape and Legitimacy.* Aldershot: Ashgate, 2001.

McCabe, Richard A. "Elizabethan Satire and the Bishop' Ban of 1599." In *Year Book of English Studies* 11 (1981): 188–93.

McClung, William A. *The Country House in English Renaissance Poetry.* Berkeley: U of California P, 1977.

McIntosh, Marjorie K. "Poverty, Charity, and Coercion in Elizabethan England." *Journal of Interdisciplinary History* 35:3 (2005): 457–79.

McMillin, Scott and Sally-Beth MacLean. *The Queen's Men and Their Plays.* Cambridge: Cambridge UP, 1998.

McMullan, John L. *The Canting Crew: London's Criminal Underworld 1550–1700.* New Brunswick: Rutgers UP, 1984.

Merchant, Paul. "Thomas Heywood's Hand in *The Seven Champions of Christendom*." *Library* 33:3 (1978): 226–30.

Montrose, Louis Adrian. "A Kingdom of Shadows." In *The Theatrical City: Culture, Theatre and Politics in London 1576–1649.* Eds. David L. Smith, Richard Strier and David Bevington. Cambridge: Cambridge UP, 1995. 68–86.

Mowat, Barbara A. "The theater and Literary Culture." In *A New History of Early English Drama.* Eds. John D. Cox & David Scott Kastan. New York: Columbia UP, 1997. 213–30.

Nauta, Ruurd R. *Poetry for Patrons: Literary Communication in the Age of Domitian.* Leiden: Brill, 2002.

Nelson, Alan H. "George Buc, William Shakespeare, and the Folger *George a Greene*." *Shakespeare Quarterly* 49 (1998): 74–83.

Nelson, Malcolm A. *The Robin Hood Tradition in the English Renaissance.* Salzburg Studies in English Literature. Salzburg: Institut für Englische Sprache und Literatur, 1973.

O'Callaghan, Michelle. *The 'Shepheards Nation': Jacobean Spenserians and Early Stuart Political Culture, 1612–1625.* Oxford: Oxford UP, 2000.

Orgel, Stephen. *Impersonations: The Performance of Gender in Shakespeare's England.* Cambridge: Cambridge UP, 1996.

Ozawa Hiroshi. "Karigi no Koromo wo Kiserarete: *Macbeth* to Ifuku no Gekijyō." In *Eibungaku to Dōtoku.* Ed. Sonoi Eisyu. Kyusyu UP, 2005. 25–38.

Palmer, Barbara D. "Early Modern Mobility: Players, Payments, and Patrons." *Shakespeare Quarterly* 56 (2005): 259–305.

Patterson, Annabel. *Shakespeare and the Popular Voice.* Oxford: Basil Blackwell, 1989.

Pettitt, Thomas. "Local and 'Customary' Drama." In *A Companion to English Renaissance Literature and Culture.* Ed. Michael Hattaway. Oxford: Blackwell, 2000. 464–76.

Pfister, Manfred. "Comic Subversion: A Bakhtinian View of the Comic in Shakespeare." *Deutsche Shakespeare Gesellschaft West Jahrbuch* (1987): 27–43.

Pound, John. *Poverty and Vagrancy in Tudor England.* 1971 rpt. London: Longman, 1982.

Purkiss, Diane. *The Witch in History: Early Modern and Twentieth-century Representations.* London and New York: Routledge, 1996.

Randall, Dale B. "'This is the Chase': or, the Further Pursuit of Shakespeare's Bear." *Shakespeare Jahrbuch* 121 (1985): 89–95.

Rathmell, J. C. A. "Jonson, Lord Lisle, and Penshurst." *English Literary Renaissance,* 1 (1971): 250–60.

Renwick, Roger deV. "The Mummers' Play and *The Old Wives Tale.*" *Journal of American Folklore.* Vol.94, No.374 (1981): 433–55.

Reynolds, George F. "*Mucedorus,* Most Popular Elizabethan Play?" In *Studies in the English Renaissance Drama.* Eds. Josephine W. Bennett et al. New York: New York UP, 1959. 248–68.

Robertson, James. "The Adventures of Dick Whittington and the Social Construction of Elizabethan London." In *Guilds, Society & Economy in London 1450–1800.* Eds. Ian Anders Gadd and Patrick Wallis. London: Centre for Metropolitan History Institute of Historical Research in Association with Guildhall Library, 2002. 51–66.

Robinson, J. W. "Palpable Hot Ice: Dramatic Burlesque in *A Midsummer-Night's Dream.*" *Studies in Philology* 61 (1964): 192–204.

Rockey, Laurilyn J. "*The Old Wives Tale* as Dramatic Satire." *Educational Theatre Journal* 22 (1970): 268–75.

Røstvig, Maren-Sofie. *The Happy Man: Studies in the Metamorphoses of a Classical Ideal,* Vol.1: 1600–1700. 2nd ed. 1954 rep. Oslo: Norwegian UP, 1962.

Sale, Carolyn. "Slanderous Aesthetics and the Woman Writer: The Case of *Hole v. White*." In *From Script to Stage in Early Modern England*. Eds. Peter Holland and Stephen Orgel. New York: Palgrave Macmillan, 2004. 181–94.

Salgado, Gamini. *The Elizabethan Underworld*. London: Book Club Associates, 1977.

Sasayama Takashi. *Dorama to Kankyaku: Kankyaku-hannoh no Kōzō to Gikyoku no Imi*. Kenkyusya, 1982.

Schneider, Jane. "Fantastical Colors in Foggy London: The New Fashion Potential of the Late Sixteenth Century." In *Material London, ca. 1600*. Ed. Lena Cowen Orlin. Philadelphia: U of Pennsylvania P, 2000. 109–27.

Seaver, Paul S. *Wallington's World: A Puritan Artisan in Seventeenth-Century London*. London: Methuen, 1985.

Singman, Jeffrey L. *Robin Hood: The Shaping of the Legend*. Westport: Greenwood, 1998.

Sisson, C. J. *Lost Plays of Shakespeare's Age*. 1936 rpt. London: Frank Cass, 1970.

Skura, Meredith. "Anthony Munday's 'Gentrification' of Robin Hood." *English Literary Renaissance* 33 (2003): 155–80.

Slack, Paul. *Poverty and Policy in Tudor and Stuart England*. London: Longman, 1988.

Smith, Steven R. "Communication the London Apprentices as Seventeenth-century Adolescents." *Past and Present* 61 (1973): 149–61.

Stallybrass, Peter. "'Drunk with the Cup of Liberty': Robin Hood, the Carnivalesque, and the Rhetoric of Violence in Early Modern England." *Semiotica* 54 (1985): 113–45.

Stevenson, Laura Caroline. *Praise and Paradox: Merchants and Craftsmen in Elizabethan Popular Literature*. Cambridge: Cambridge UP, 1984.

Stokes, James D. "The Wells Cordwainers Show: New Evidence Concerning Guild Entertainments in Somerset." *Comparative Drama* 19.4 (1985–1986): 332–46.

---. "Robin Hood and the Churchwardens in Yeovil." *Medieval & Renaissance Drama in England* 3 (1986): 1–25.

---. "The Wells Shows of 1607." In *Festive Drama: Papers from the 6th Triennial Colloquium of the International Society for the Study of Medieval Theatre Lancaster, 13–19 July, 1987*. Ed. Meg Twycross. Cambridge: D. S. Brewer, 1996. 145–56.

---. "Bull and Bear Baiting in Somerset: The Gentles' Sport." In *English Parish Drama*. Eds. Alexandra F. Johnston & Wim Hüsken. Amsterdam: Atlanta, GA, 1996. 64–80.

---. "Processional Entertainments in Villages and Small Towns." In *Moving Subjects: Processional Performance in the Middle Ages and the Renaissance*.

Eds. Kathleen Ashley and Wim Hüsken. Amsterdam: Atlanta GA, 2001. 239–57.

Strong, Roy C. "The Popular Celebration of the Accession Day of Queen Elizabeth I." *Journal of the Warburg and Courtauld Institutes* 21 (1958): 86–103.

---. *The Cult of Elizabeth: Elizabethan Portraiture and Pageantry.* London: Thames & Hudson, 1977.

Suzuki Zenzō. *Igirisu Fūshibungaku no Keifu.* Kenkyusha, 1996.

Tardif, Richard. "The 'Mistery' of Robin Hood: A New Social Context for the Texts." In *Words and Worlds: Studies in the Social Role of Verbal Culture.* Eds. Stephen Knight and S. N. Mukherjee. Sydney Studies in Society and Culture No. 1. Sydney: Sydney Association for Studies in Society and Culture, 1983. 130–45.

Thomas, Keith. *Religion and the Decline of Magic.* 1971 rpt. London: Penguin, 1991.

---. *Rule and Misrule in the Schools of Early Modern England.* Reading: U of Reading, 1976.

---. "The Place of Laughter in Tudor and Stuart England." *TLS* January 21 (1977): 77–81.

---. *Man and the Natural World: Changing Attitude in England 1500–1800.* London: Penguin, 1983.

Thornberry, Richard T. "A Seventeenth-Century Revival of *Mucedorus* in London before 1610." *Shakespeare Quarterly* 28 (1977): 362–64.

Tiddy, R. J. E. *The Mummers' Play.* Oxford: Clarendon P, 1923.

Twycross, Meg. "Some Approaches to Dramatic Festivity, Especially Processions." In *Festive Drama: Papers from the 6th Triennial Colloquium of the International Society for the Study of Medieval Theatre Lancaster, 13–19 July, 1987.* Ed. Meg Twycross. Cambridge: D. S. Brewer, 1996. 1–33.

Twycross, Meg and Sarah Carpenter. *Masks and Masking in Medieval and Early Tudor England.* Aldershot: Ashgate, 2002.

Unwin, George. *The Gilds and Companies of London.* London: Frank Cass, 1966.

Wasson, John. "The End of an Era: Parish Drama in England from 1520 to the Dissolution." *Research Opportunities in Renaissance Drama* 31 (1992):70–78.

Wayne, Don E. *Penshurst: the Semiotics of Place and the Poetics of History.* London: Methuen, 1984.

Weimann, Robertt. *Shakespeare and the Popular Tradition in the Theater: Studies in the Social Dimension of Dramatic Form and Function.* Baltimore: Johns Hopkins UP, 1978.

Welsford, Enid. *The Fool: His Social and Literary History.* 1935 rpt. Gloucester: Peter Smith, 1966.

Westfall, Suzanne. "'What Revels are in Hand?': Performances in the Great Households." In *A Companion to Renaissance Drama*. Ed. Arthur F. Kinney. Oxford: Blackwell, 2002. 266–80.

Wickham, Glynne. *The Medieval Theatre*. 1974 rpt. London: Weidenfeld and Nicolson, 1977.

Wiles, David. *The Early Plays of Robin Hood*. Cambridge: D. S. Brewer, 1981.

---. "'That Day are You Free': *The Shoemakers Holiday*." *Cahiers Elisabéthains* 38 (1990): 49–60.

Williams, Penry. "Shakespeare's *A Midsummer Night's Dream*: Social Tensions Contained." In *The Theatrical City: Culture, Theatre and Politics in London 1576–1649*. Eds. David L. Smith, Richard Strier and David Bevington. Cambridge: Cambridge UP, 1995. 55–67.

Williams, Raymond. *The Country and the City*. London: Chatto & Windus, 1973.

Withington, Robert. *English Pageantry: An Historical Outline*. Vol. 1. 1918 rpt. New York: Arno P, 1980.

Woodbridge, Linda. "The Peddler and the Pawn: Why Did Tudor England Consider Peddlers to Be Rogues?" In *Rogues and Early Modern English Culture*. Eds. Craig Dionne and Steve Mentz. Ann Arbor: U of Michigan P, 2004. 143–70.

Wright, Louis B. *Middle-Class Culture in Elizabethan England*. Chapel Hill: U of North Carolina P, 1935.

Wrightson, Keith. *English Society 1580–1680*. London: Hutchinson, 1982.

Yates, Frances A. *Astraea: The Imperial Theme in the Sixteenth Century*. London: Routledge & Kegan Paul, 1975.

Young, Steven C. *The Frame Structure in Tudor and Stuart Drama*. Salzburg: U of Salzburg, 1974.

Index

A

ales 14, 50-51, 107-108, 120
alms 21, 39, 52-53, 54, 65, 69, 107
Apuleius 59
Ash Wednesday 106, 122

B

ballads 72-73, 75, 76, 77, 78, 84, 85, 88, 90, 95, 97-98, 101, 122, 127
Barber, C. L. 7, 11, 13, 15, 16, 17, 61, 62
  Shakespeare's Festive Comedies 7, 15-17, 61-62
Bakhtin, Mikhail 17
  Rabelais and His World 17
bearbaiting 39, 119, 120
Beaumont and Fletcher 26
  The Knight of the Burning Pestle 80, 84
beggars 36, 39-40, 53, 64, 110- 112, 126
Binnie, Patricia 44, 52, 53, 55, 56
the Bishop's Ban 32
The Book of Common Prayer 21, 68
Books of Homilies 21, 54
Brathwaite, Richard 81, 82
  A Strappado for the Diuell 81-82
Breton, Nicholas 23, 40
  "Eleuen of the Clocke" 40
  Fantastickes 23
  A Merrie Dialogve betwixt The Taker and Mistaker 112
Bristol, Michael 17, 18, 121, 122, 125
  Carnival and Theatre 17
  "In Search of the Bear" 121-122, 125
brothels 105, 113-118
burlesque 26, 46, 57

C

The Canterbury Tales 50, 60
Carew, Thomas 28, 38
  "To Saxham" 28
Catholic 12, 13, 14, 68
charity 38-39, 52-55, 60, 67-68, 73, 107
  see also hospitality
chimneys 31-33
chorus 7, 9, 61, 63, 100, 105-107, 118, 124, 126
Christmas 11, 16, 21-26, 36-37, 41, 48, 49, 51-52, 55, 62, 67, 68-69, 107, 121-122
The Christmas Prince 16
The Cobler of Caunterburie 50, 60
the Cockpit 78, 85, 93, 97
Cope, Jackson I 45, 55
the Cordwainers Show 80-81
Corpus Christi 13
country house poems 27-32, 34, 38, 40, 63
Cox, John D. 45, 49
cross-dressing 9, 128-129

D

Dekker, Thomas 33, 34, 40, 82, 96
  A Shoemaker's Holiday 82, 85
  A Strange Horse-Race 33, 34
Deloney, Thomas 82, 83
  The Gentle Craft 82
  Jack of Newbury 83
  Thomas of Reading 83
Elizabeth I 13, 14, 35
ember-eve 107

F

festivals   11-26, 37, 46, 51, 61, 62, 67, 105, 127
Frazer, James G.   18
   The Golden Bough   18
Frye, Northrop   15

G

gentry   20, 32-36, 38, 40, 65, 67, 69, 87, 99, 128
   see also nobility
George a Greene   71, 72-73, 75-87, 92
the Globe   87, 93, 94, 103, 106, 126
the Golden Age   14, 28-29, 55, 89-90, 99, 112
Greene, Robert   32, 40, 43, 65, 72, 73, 128
   Orlando Furioso   43
   Pandosto   123-124
   A Quip for an Vpstart Courtier   32-33, 40-41, 65, 128
guilds   14, 79-81, 84-85, 86

H

Hall, Joseph   31, 32
   "House-keeping's Dead"   31
   Virgidemiae   31-32
harvest   21, 22-23, 29, 47, 55, 65-66
Heal, Felicity   20, 21, 24, 34, 35, 53, 63, 66, 68
   "The Crown, the Gentry and London"   35-36
   Hospitality in Early Modern England   20-21, 24, 35, 53, 66
   "The Idea of Hospitality in Early Modern England"   20-21, 34, 53
   Of Prelates and Princes   63, 68
   "The Archbishops of Canterbury and the Practice of Hospitality"   63
Henry VIII   13, 64
Henslowe, Philip   72, 95

Herrick, Robert   31, 38, 50
   "Twelfe Night, or King and Queene" in *Hesperides*   50-51
   A Panegyric to Sir Lewis Pemberton   31
Heywood, Thomas   78, 84, 94, 96, 97, 100
   The Fair Maid of the West   100
   The Golden Age   97, 100-101
   The Silver Age   97
   The Late Lancashire Witches   94
Hibbard, G. R.   34
Hook, Frank S.   44, 55, 59
Horace   32, 58, 58
   Eighth Satire   32
hospitality   20-40, 52-54, 62-63, 65-70, 77, 83, 87, 99, 107-111, 112, 122
   see also charity
households   20, 24, 27, 29, 32-33
household entertainment   45, 47-48, 49, 56-57
housekeeping   22, 29, 31-32, 34, 35, 37, 41, 69

J

James I   35, 36, 37, 38, 62
   Basilikon Doron   37
   A Declaration of Sports   37-38
   "An Elegy Written by the King"   36
Johnson, Richard   83, 84, 93, 95, 96, 97, 98
   A Crowne-Garland of Govlden Roses   84, 95-96
   The Most Famous History of the Seauen Champions of Christendom   93, 96
   Nine Worthies of London   83
Jonson, Ben   27, 29, 31, 34, 36, 38, 94, 101
   Bartholomew Fair   94-95, 101
   The New Inne   101
   "To Penshurst"   27-31, 34, 36, 38
   "To Sir Robert Wroth"   29
   The Forest   27, 38
   Epigrams   27, 29, 38
Juvenal   31, 58
   Fifth Satire   31

K

the King's Men 73, 87, 93, 100
Knights, L. C. 33-34

L

lamb's wool 51-53
Lancashire witches 94
landlords 27, 29, 31-32, 34, 36, 38
Laroque, François 11, 14, 25, 26, 71, 88, 120-121
  "Pagan Ritual, Christian Liturgy, and Folk Customs in *The Winter's Tale*" 121
  Shakespeare's Festive World 11, 14, 25, 26, 71, 88
Lent 106, 107, 122
liberality 62-63, 65
  see also hospitality
The Life of Lazarillo de Tormes 60
Look About You 75
the Lord Admiral's Men 72, 73, 82
Lord Mayor of London 82, 83, 95
Lord Mayor's Show 84, 88
the Lord of Misrule 15-16, 20, 23
Lucian 18, 58, 59
  Ta pros Kronon / Saturnalia 18-19

M

Martial 29, 30, 34
  Epigrams 29-30, 138n11
Mary I 13
May festivities and games 11-12, 46, 71, 80-81, 101
maypoles 12, 13, 14
Menippean satire 57-59, 60
A Merry Knack to Know a Knave 69-70
meta-theatrical devices 45, 56-57
Middleton, Thomas 113
  A Chaste Maid in Cheapside 113, 114

Midsummer Day 11, 14, 80
Midsummer shows 56
Midsummer Watch 13, 88
Morris dance 11, 14, 64
Mucedorus 71, 73-75, 80, 87-93, 97, 98, 99
Mummer's plays 55-56
Mumming 46
Munday, Anthony 72, 75, 78, 96
  The Death of Robert Earl of Huntington 75
  The Downfall of Robert Earl of Huntington 72, 75

N

Nashe, Thomas 8, 11, 25, 61, 63, 64, 69
  Summer's Last Will and Testament 8, 11, 25-26, 41, 61-70
neighbors 22, 39, 40, 53, 68, 107, 123, 124
New Historicists 17-18, 45
nobility 20, 32, 38, 40, 41, 62-63, 67, 68-69, 91, 99, 128
  see also gentry

O

offstage reality 7, 9, 12, 41, 61, 105, 111, 122, 130

P

parishes 12, 14, 21, 40, 48, 53, 54-55, 73, 74, 87, 107, 110, 111, 120
pastoral 11, 25, 26, 36, 38, 99, 119, 120-121, 126-127
patrons 32, 34, 38, 40, 47, 57, 60, 61, 63, 66-67, 69
Paul, George 66, 69
  The Life of John Whitgift 67

Peele, George   43, 45, 52, 55, 59
    Edward I   75
    The Old Wives Tale   8, 41, 43-45, 49-60, 63, 70, 71
Petronius   32, 59
    Satyricon   32, 59-60
Phister, Manfred   17-18
The Pinner of Wakefield   80-81
plague   44, 61
A Pleasaunt Satyre or Poesie: Wherein is Discouered the Catholicon of Spayne, and the Chiefe Leaders of the League   58-59, 60
Plough Monday   11, 14, 121
play-within-a play   45-47
the poor   18-22, 32-33, 35, 39, 48-49, 53-55, 64-69, 77, 83
    relief   35-36, 39-40, 53, 55, 107-108, 110
Poor Robins Hue and Cry after Good House-Keeping   41
prostitution   113-114, 117
Protestant culture   12-14, 24
provincial performances   44-45, 57
Puritans   13, 26, 62, 108, 125, 128

Q

the Queen's Men   43-45, 97
Questions of Profitable and Pleasant Concernings   25, 125-126

R

the Red Bull   78, 83, 93, 95, 97, 100
Reformation   13-14, 17, 26
    post-   24
Robin Hood   71, 73
Robin Hood plays   9, 48, 57, 73, 75-76, 77-78, 87
the Rose   72, 78, 81, 82, 85, 93
Rowley, William   82-83
    A Shoemaker, A Gentleman   83

royal proclamations   35-38
Rych, Barnabee   112, 114, 129
    The Honestie of This Age   112-113, 114, 129

S

Saint George   47, 71, 95-96, 98, 101
Saint George's Day   11, 14, 88
Saint George plays   47, 48-49, 56, 57, 64, 88, 95-96, 97
Saturnalia   7, 15-20, 24, 45, 47, 55, 59, 82
satire   9, 31-32, 34, 60, 63, 64, 66, 67, 69, 93, 111, 117, 118, 122
The Seven Champions of Christendom   9, 71, 93-101, 126
Shakespeare, William   7, 9, 45, 46, 72, 93, 100, 103, 104, 126
    Cymbeline   101
    Henry V   100
    Love's Labor's Lost   16, 50
    A Midsummer Night's Dream   16, 45-49, 50, 56
    Pericles   9, 101, 103-118
    The Tempest   100
    Twelfth Night   16, 52
    The Winter's Tale   7, 9, 11, 24-25, 26, 100, 119-132
sheep-shearing   7, 11, 24-25
Shrove Tuesday   11, 82, 85, 121, 122
Smith, Wentworth   95
    The Hector of Germany   95
social classes   19, 34, 38, 40, 66, 69, 87, 90, 101, 105, 126, 127
Statius   19
    The Kalends of December   19-20
story-telling framework   9, 45, 49, 56-57, 60
Stow, John   16, 79
    A Survey of London   16, 79
strangers   22-23, 39-40, 49, 53, 67, 70
Strong, Roy   14
Stubbes, Philip   12, 13, 16
    The Anatomie of Abuses   12-13, 128

Sumptuary Laws of Apparel 128-129

T

Tibullus 29
   Elegy 29, 138n10
Tudor Interludes 56-57
Tusser, Thomas 21, 23, 26, 30
   Five Hundred Points of Good Husbandry 21-23, 26, 30, 41
   A Hundredth Goode Pointes of Husbandrie 21
Twelfth Night 11, 50-52
Twine, Laurence 104, 109, 115
   The Patterne of Painfull Adventures 104-105, 109, 115

V

Virgil 29
   Georgics 29, 138n9

W

wassail 51
Whitgift, John, archbishop of Canterbury 61, 63, 66-67, 68, 69
Wickham, Glynne 11, 26, 71
   The Medieval Theatre 26
a wild man 88
Wilkin, George 103, 104, 109
   The Painfull Aduentures of Pericles, Prince of Tyre 103, 104, 109
Williams, Raymond 34
Wilson, Robert 69
   The Coblers Prophesie 69
   The Three Ladies of London 69
   The Three Lords and Three Ladies of London 69
Whittington, Sir Richard 83-84

Y

Yates, Frances A. 14
yeomans 65-66, 86
Young, Steven C. 52

著者略歴

前原 澄子 （まえはら・すみこ）

1995年　The University of Reading, M.A. in the English Renaissance修了
2006年　関西学院大学大学院文学研究科英文学専攻博士課程後期過程修了
現　在　国立明石工業高等専門学校　一般科目教授

Festive Romances in Early Modern Drama:
Nostalgia for Ancient Hospitality
and Wish-fulfillment Fantasy in Mobile Society

2009年8月20日　初版第一刷発行

著　者　前原澄子
発行者　宮原浩二郎
発行所　関西学院大学出版会
所在地　〒662-0891 兵庫県西宮市上ケ原一番町1-155
電　話　0798-53-7002

印　刷　協和印刷株式会社

©Sumiko Maehara 2009
Printed in Japan by Kwansei Gakuin University Press
ISBN 978-4-86283-044-9
乱丁・落丁本はお取り替えいたします。
本書の全部または一部を無断で複写・複製することを禁じます。
http://www.kwansei.ac.jp/press